PIGEON FO[RK] BUT WE[?] OF CHARACTERS—AND KILLERS.

Eunice Krebbs: Cordelia's sister must have been pretty once—before her husband started using her as a doormat. But a trace of Turley pride kept her insisting that Grammy had been only a tad forgetful . . .

Joe Eddy Krebbs: 300 pounds of mean, Joe Eddy told me flat out that "Grammy's train had slipped the tracks." I kind of hoped he was the one who did Grammy in . . .

Grampap Turley: It was obvious he'd worshipped Grammy—and been a mite afraid of her. Why, he still wouldn't dare throw out her seed catalogue . . .

Delbert Sims: The town drunk—or one of them, anyway— he played cards with Eunice, Joe Eddy, and Grandpappy the night Grammy was killed. When he said he hadn't seen Joe Eddy since, I knew he was lying . . .

Emmaline Johnston: She kept writing to the *Pigeon Fork Gazette* about the murdered pets—even after the threatening notes began showing up in her mailbox. Then someone poisoned Fluffy, one of her twelve cats . . .

Sheriff Vergil Minrath: He'd been on the case for seven months with no results—and no interference. I had it for one day when someone slashed my tires. I thought Vergil would bust a gut from jealousy . . .

PET PEEVES

Taylor McCafferty

POCKET BOOKS

New York   London   Toronto   Sydney   Tokyo   Singapore

An *Original* Publication of POCKET BOOKS

POCKET BOOKS, a division of Simon & Schuster Inc.
1230 Avenue of the Americas, New York, NY 10020

ISBN: 0-671-72802-4

First Pocket Books printing October 1990

10 9 8 7 6 5 4 3 2 1

For my husband, John,
my twin sister, Beverly,
and my three pet peeves,
Geoff, Chris, and Rachael

PET
PEEVES

CHAPTER

ONE

It's tough being a hard-boiled detective in a small town. For one thing, I think it's pretty much a requirement for the job that you have a neon sign across from your office, and venetian blinds on your office windows. That way, at night, the sign can blink off and on, casting long, melancholy, striped shadows across your desk. You need that kind of atmosphere if you're going to stay hard-boiled.

Here in Pigeon Fork, Kentucky, we don't have even one neon sign. Unless you count that dinky little thing that hangs in the window of Frank's Bar and Grill. It's bright red, and it spells out "Say Bull," and it's so small, it's not going to be casting any shadows even if my office were across the street. Which it isn't.

My office is over my brother Elmo's drugstore. This is pretty convenient, since during slow times I told Elmo I'd help out down there by cleaning up and running the soda fountain. To tell you the truth, in Pigeon Fork slow times are Monday through Saturday. It would be slow on Sunday, too, but Sundays I and Elmo's are closed.

I used to feel downright irritated about things being so quiet and all. These days, however, I'm real grateful. After all the fuss about them pet murders, quiet feels real good.

Of course, I didn't feel this way at all a few months ago. That September Tuesday when Cordelia Turley sashayed her way into my life, things had been so slow for so long that I was actually beginning to consider going into another line of work. Something a little more fast-paced. Say, plumbing, for instance. I was mulling this over in my mind while I was mopping Elmo's floor.

One of the Hawley kids had just been in, and he'd dropped his chocolate ice-cream cone smack dab in the middle of the antacids aisle. That cone was making my mop a sticky mess. I must've said every curse word I knew under my breath, and I was trying real hard to think up some new ones, when Melba Hawley interrupted me. "Haskell, hey, Haskell," she said.

Melba Hawley is Elmo's less-than-efficient secretary/bookkeeper, which means she spends a lot of her time looking out the window. I glanced over at her, and—no surprise—she was peering out the front window as usual. "Haskell," she said, "I think you got yourself a customer."

"Client, Melba," I corrected her, for what must've been the hundredth time.

Melba just looked at me blankly.

"We call them clients," I said.

"La dee da," she said, and turned back to the window.

I followed her glance, and sure enough, it did look like somebody was climbing the stairs to my office. I

2

didn't recognize the woman, but that didn't mean anything anymore. Ever since they put in the new interstate, there've been a lot of new faces in town.

Even from where I stood, I could see that this particular new face belonged to what I call a Pigeon Fork 10. Anywhere else in the United States, she probably would've been a 7 or an 8, but here in Pigeon Fork a whole lot of the women are still wearing their hair in beehives. They're also still wearing clothes you haven't seen anywhere else in about twenty years, and most of the women look as if they could lift the front end of a pickup truck. And, maybe, drop it on you.

So, here indeed was a 10 to my thirsty eyes. Melba must've noticed how my face brightened, because right away she started patting at her brown beehive, smoothing down any stray hairs. "Well, my goodness, Haskell, you certainly look awfully eager—"

I didn't stay to hear the rest of it. Melba Hawley has five kids ranging from three to thirteen like stair steps. Since Otis Hawley saw fit to up and die two years ago, she's been glancing my way real often. Of course, she's been glancing every other eligible man's way, too. Unfortunately, poor Melba is lugging around about one hundred extra pounds—quite a few of which she sits on—and her five kids could make Art Linkletter want to slap them. After getting to know Melba (at work only, mind you) and meeting her five hellions, it is my opinion that in Otis Hawley's case, that old joke is true. Otis didn't die. He's hiding.

I almost ran out the front door of Elmo's Drugstore. The Pigeon Fork 10 had almost gotten to the top of the stairs by then; and watching her finish going up those last few steps made me real sorry I hadn't been there for the entire climb.

She was wearing a short, navy blue suit that had one of them skinny skirts with a long slit in the back. So that when she moved at all, you could catch a glimpse of how really perfect her long legs were. I actually had to swallow once before I spoke, to make sure my voice didn't come out as a squeak. "Miss?" I said. "Are you looking for Haskell Blevins? The detective?" If she wasn't, I seriously considered pretending to be anybody she named.

She turned toward me, looking confused; and I could see now that not only were her legs very nice, but that there were quite a few things of hers that bordered on perfection. "Why, that's right," she said, "is he—? Are you—?"

I nodded. "I am."

She smiled then, still looking a little bewildered, looking back uncertainly at the drugstore I'd just come running out of. Struck by the full force of that sweet smile, I had to try three or four times to get the door to my office open.

Maybe it was taking so long to get in my own door, or the way I almost knocked over one of my lamps when I was pulling out a chair for her, but she started looking even more uncertain once she sat down in my office.

Melba calls my office "The Bermuda Rectangle." She claims it looks as if some mysterious force had pulled papers and folders and pencils from miles away onto every square inch of space. Melba is exaggerating. She is.

But from the look on my Pigeon Fork 10's face, you wouldn't have thought it. She squirmed a little in her chair, her big blue eyes growing larger by the second as they traveled around my office. Finally, she took a deep breath and said, "Actually, Mister Blevins, you're not quite what I was expecting."

She had the kind of voice you pour over pancakes. I smiled easily, and said, "Oh, that's okay. I'll work for you, anyway."

My boyish charm evidently wasn't making the impression I'd hoped. Pigeon's face reddened a little, and she looked away before she said, "I really have the most awful problem, and I think it's going to take a real"—here she paused, searching for the right word—"a real *professional*."

Now that stung. I drew myself up as tall as I could—considering that I was sitting down—and I started rattling off some of the cases I've solved in the last five years: the Stomes murder, the Hazelip extortion scandal, the Vittitow fraud, not to mention more than a few robberies here and there.

I saved the Collins kidnapping for last, because I knew she was most likely to have heard about that one. It was on national news for quite a while—in fact, practically the whole time the little girl was missing. It was one of the first cases I'd ever solved singlehandedly.

I was still back in Louisville then. Old Man Collins did appear to be a tad more grateful that I'd saved him from paying the $5 million ransom than he did that I'd brought him back a right cute little girl. Of course, I didn't tell the Pigeon Fork 10 that. I mainly dwelt on how cute that little Collins girl was. Short blond curls, dimpled cheeks, big blue eyes. And spoiled rotten. She had wanted me to drop by a toy store on the way home.

I didn't tell Pigeon that part, either. By the time I stopped to take a breath, Pigeon was looking at me a little different. But not different enough. You could tell she was still hesitant. For one thing, she said, "I—I don't know—" That's a real tip-off.

I knew then what the problem was. It's what the problem always is at first, whenever I meet a new client. People come up here looking for Peter Gunn, and they end up with me—an ordinary-looking guy with red hair. Average height, average build.

To be honest, there have also been those who have suggested that I bear a remarkable resemblance to Howdy Doody. I'm hoping that these particular people are just being cruel, and that it isn't actually true.

What is true, I admit, is that Howdy and I do have one thing in common. Freckles. People just don't take you seriously if you've got a lot of freckles. It's like they think your IQ drops a couple of notches for every freckle you've got. In my case, if that were true, my IQ would be in the minus.

So, I leaned across my desk, staring at her real seriouslike, and started in heavy with the rest of my sales pitch. I've got it memorized, I've had to say the same thing so many times. I told her how I spent eight years with Homicide in Louisville, how many hundreds of cases I worked on there, dwelling heavily on the considerably fewer that we solved. By the time I'd finished, I sounded like God's gift to crime-stopping.

I told her almost everything about those years, except how sick I got of the whole scene. I got real tired of seeing people at their worst. Believe me, when you're working Homicide, you don't run into very many nice people.

I also left out the part where Old Man Collins insisted on giving me a fat reward for finding his granddaughter. It was no doubt just pocket change to the Collinses, but it was a pretty substantial sum to me. Enough for me to buy me a house. And enough for me to do something else. Something I'd been wanting to do for a long, long time.

Don't let anybody kid you. You know all those people who come into some extra money and then say they're going to keep on working at the same job they've always had? They're lying.

I was planning my resignation speech a heartbeat after Old Man Collins pressed that cashier's check into my hand. Right after that, I hightailed it back to Pigeon Fork where I grew up. Back home where I belonged.

I knew exactly what I wanted to do once I got here. At the ripe old age of thirty-three, I wanted to own my own business—a detective agency, of course, just like I'd been dreaming about for years. I opened me an office right away, and I started waiting for the business to come pouring in.

And I kept waiting.

It's been over four months now, and up until Pigeon walked in, the toughest case I've had has been who stole the feedsacks in front of Toomey's Hardware Store. At least, Pigeon here looked a lot better than Toomey.

Evidently, I'd told her enough. When I paused for breath this time, she said, "Mister Blevins, you sound like just what I need."

I smiled real wide at that one.

She hurried on. "Something awful has happened to my grandmother." She stopped for a minute, and then added, "And to her cat and her parakeet."

I just stared at her. I had just gone through my heavy sales pitch for this? Maybe this case wasn't going to be any better than the Feedsack Caper.

The range of awful things that could possibly have happened to a grandmother and her assorted pets seemed distinctly limited. And about as interesting as paint drying. "What happened to them?" I asked.

7

Pigeon's eyes got even bigger. "They were murdered!"

This possibility had not been included in my range. "All of them?" I asked.

Pigeon nodded mutely.

"Your grandmother?"

Pigeon nodded again.

"And her cat?"

Another nod.

"*And* her bird?"

This last nod was the most vigorous of all.

I tried not to look too excited, but I was pretty sure by the last nod that I knew the case she was talking about. My heart actually started to pound. How many cases could there be involving little old ladies and pets? This one had been on the news, and in the paper for a while, and just last month it had been splattered all over the front page of one of them tabloids you can't help but read when you're checking out of the grocery.

I remembered the headline: MANIAC SLAYS GRAND-MOTHER AND PETS!!! A small headline underneath the larger one screamed, FIEND KILLED EVERYTHING THAT MOVED!

It had been the first time Pigeon Fork, Kentucky, had made national news. I distinctly remember not feeling proud.

If I was right, this was the sort of case that could make a reputation. It could put you on the detecting map, so to speak. Whoever solved this case was going to get all the free publicity he could stand. And, if it happened to be me, I'd have clients coming from all over Crayton County. I might actually get too busy to mop Elmo's floor.

I was almost sure, but I asked anyway, "You don't mean the Turley murder?"

I wished right away I had said "case," instead of "murder," because tears appeared in the big blue eyes in front of me. They blinked a couple of times, and then Pigeon said, "Mrs. Turley was my grandmother. I'm Cordelia Turley."

I mumbled something like "I'm so sorry," feeling clumsy. I never do know what to say to somebody who's lost somebody they evidently cared about. Particularly if it was murder.

Cordelia blinked again, and went on. "I live in Nashville, and I've been waiting and waiting for them to catch who did this awful thing. But it's been months now. Seven whole months! And they still haven't caught this—this—" She paused, looking for the right word again.

"Fiend?" I offered.

She nodded, causing her short brown curls to bob charmingly about her face. "That's right," she said. "Fiend." She made it sound as if it had two syllables. Fah-heend.

She hurried on to tell me the rest of it. Her grandparents had been living way out on the edge of town, and from the way it sounded, smack-dab in the middle of nowhere. Next door, equally in the middle of nowhere, lived Cordelia's sister, Eunice, and her husband, Joe Eddy Krebbs. The Krebbses had moved out there about a year ago, when her grandmother's only neighbor had put his house up for sale. "Eunice had been wanting to move closer to Grammy for some time," Cordelia said.

I just looked at her. Up until now, I hadn't connected the name, but back in high school I'd known a Eunice Turley. Was it *her* grandmother who'd been killed? I'd also known a Joe Eddy Krebbs back then, too. Both Joe Eddy and Eunice were two years behind me, so I didn't know either one of them real well. I did remember, though, that Eunice was a right pretty little thing— and that Joe Eddy was not. As I recall, Joe Eddy got even less pretty as time went by, getting his nose broke every so often playing on the high school football team.

As Cordelia went on, I looked at her even more closely. She had to be at least four years younger than me. Maybe that's why I didn't remember her— Cordelia was too many grades behind me.

"Eunice thought that living close to Grammy would be a good idea," Cordelia was going on, "being as how Grammy and Grampap are getting on up in years."

Here it seemed to occur to Cordelia suddenly that Grammy wasn't getting on up in years any longer, and she broke off. Once again, I was looking at tears in those big blue eyes.

Once again, I sat there like a bump on a pickle, trying to think up something to say. I'd already used "I'm sorry," and that did seem to pretty much cover it. What else was there to say? It's nice that Grammy had had such a long life? Somehow, that seemed to ignore the unfortunate way the poor woman had died. I was thinking of comforting remarks—and discarding them—when Cordelia brushed her tears away and continued, "And, to be honest, I guess Grammy was really showing her age this last year or so."

"Oh?" Mentally, I congratulated myself for thinking of a quick reply this time. No hesitation at all.

Cordelia reddened. "It wasn't much, just every once in a while poor Grammy would wear her skirt inside out. Things like that. And, sometimes, she'd forget what she was doing, right in the middle of doing it."

Grammy didn't sound any too tightly wrapped; but then again, she didn't sound much more out of it than, say, me, for instance. I'd put on my sweater inside out a few times myself. If that qualified you for the looney bin, I was in trouble.

I didn't tell Cordelia that, though. Hearing about my problems with sweaters on top of the freckles would probably send her running right out of my office, screaming.

"Oh, my," I said. I was getting to be a real conversationalist.

"Yes," Cordelia said, shaking her head. "Poor Grammy was having a few problems, but she was all right. She just needed a little help, sometimes."

"Hmm," I said. I hoped I looked sympathetic. "Now, on the night in question—" I said, hoping to get her off the subject of inside-out clothes.

"Yes, well—" Cordelia was silent again. Blinking furiously.

This time, having already decided there was really nothing one could say, I went with what was safe. I said nothing.

Eventually, Cordelia—with quite a few pauses—told me what had happened. The night her poor Grammy was killed, Cordelia's grandfather and a friend of his by the name of Delbert Sims and Eunice's husband were all over at Eunice's house, playing cards. No one heard or saw anything unusual. Then, about one-thirty in the morning, the game broke up. Delbert Sims went on home, and Grampap did the same.

Grampap, however, didn't stay home long. The old man came running back in about one minute, tops, white as a sheet, screaming and crying that Grammy was dead. He'd found her lying on the kitchen floor, right next to her cat and her parakeet, equally dead.

"That's—that's all I know," Cordelia finished. "The sheriff said it looked as though all of them had been hit with a—with a—"

"Blunt object?" I offered gently. I remembered this from the newspaper accounts I'd read. The old woman, the cat, and the bird had all been clobbered with something heavy. The police, however, weren't at all sure what this something heavy could be. They never had located the weapon.

Cordelia nodded, her eyes huge. "Oh, Haskell, you've got to help me find out who did this awful thing!"

I tried to look confident, but I couldn't help wondering. What would I be able to find out that the police hadn't already? I smiled, anyway, and promised to go see Cordelia's sister and brother-in-law right away. Then, clearing my throat, I said, "My fees are kinda steep. I charge $30 an hour, or $200 a day."

Actually, as far as some detective agencies go, I could've been having a sale. In fact, I've considered putting out a sign that says, "Haskell Blevins, Discount Detective." But, around here, people think I'm charging an arm and a leg. And maybe a torso or two. You tell somebody from Pigeon Fork you want $30 an hour for doing detective work, and you get an argument. Or laughter.

This is another reason why I was thinking earlier about plumbing as a new career. Around these parts, plumbers make more per hour than I do. And people don't laugh, either. Plumbing they take seriously.

Cordelia, however, didn't bat an eye at my rate. She just looked straight at me, and said, "Mr. Blevins, when Grammy died, I inherited $10,000 in life insurance. I didn't even know Grammy had named me as beneficiary. I'll spend every penny of that money, if I have to, to find out who did this to her."

I nodded. This was one sweet little lady. "Everybody calls me Haskell."

"Haskell, then," she added, smiling.

She reached for her purse just as a small frown flickered across her face. Like a cloud scooting across a flawless sky. "Now, I—I don't have the money yet. They say it'll be any day now, though." She pulled out her checkbook and a ballpoint pen. "But I'll write you a check for $100 right this minute—to start you off."

Even the handwriting on that check looked pretty.

Cordelia started to get up to leave, but I had one more question for her. "Did anyone else do any inheriting?"

"Eunice and I both did," she said. "Grammy evidently took out a $10,000 insurance policy for each of her grandkids. Wasn't that sweet?" Cordelia was blinking again, her voice choked with emotion.

I didn't say anything. I just nodded, smiling. It was either real sweet—or real dumb. One or the other.

CHAPTER
TWO

I was wrong about Eunice and Joe Eddy Krebbs living in the middle of nowhere. I'd been driving almost thirty minutes, and I was pretty sure I'd already passed nowhere several miles back when I saw a dirt road finally turning off to my left.

Five miles later, after eating about forty pounds of dust—and watching the front end of my brand-new Ford pickup bounce like a jack-in-the-box over pothole after pothole—I pulled up to a small white frame house badly in need of paint. In back of the house stood a small barn in even worse need.

From where I was sitting, it looked like Eunice and Joe Eddy would have no trouble finding a use for a spare ten grand.

The house next door didn't look any better. In fact, it looked a lot worse. It was painted Pepto Bismol pink—a color that appropriately made your stomach churn the minute you saw it.

The Pepto Bismol house was not twenty steps away from the white frame, believe it or not. This is something you see a lot out in these parts, and I might as well admit it, I've never been able to understand the logic here.

You've got a house miles away from the city, out so far in the boonies that you're sure its owner must've moved all the way out here to make sure he got himself an ample dose of privacy. And yet, likely as not, you'll have another house built right next to the first, as close as if they'd both been in a subdivision smack-dab in the middle of the city.

As my dad used to say, go figure.

I'd called Eunice to tell her I was coming, being as how I was not at all inclined to drive over thirty miles to an empty house. So Eunice knew I was on my way.

For some reason, though, she had not seen fit to tie up her dog. As soon as I got out of my truck, this bundle of bones lightly sprinkled with brown fur came tearing around the side of the house, teeth showing yellowy white against a dark brown, very angry face.

"Good dog, good dog," I said. "Good dog." Apparently, however, he'd already made up his mind on the subject. And "good" was not what this creature was aiming for.

He made a wild grab for my ankles just as Eunice appeared at the front door. I just got a fleeting glimpse of her, though. The first glimpse she had of me was my backside, beating a hasty retreat back to my truck. I beat the brown monster by a good half a second, slamming the door in its snarling little face.

The dog looked insulted. It ran around my truck twice, looking for a way to get in, and then unable to clamp its molars around something attached to me personally, it decided to attack the metal surrounding me. It threw its skinny body again and again against the door on the passenger side. I sat there, hoping it knocked itself senseless, hearing the unmistakable sounds of dog claws raking mercilessly against what had recently been a very nice paint job. Midnight blue with a metallic flake.

"Down, Hector, now, down, boy." The thin, pale woman who was now walking slowly over to my truck needed a course in assertiveness training. I stared at her. *This* was Eunice? The pretty girl I remembered from high school? Good heavens, what had happened? This woman still had the old Eunice's even features, but she looked as if she'd been left in the rinse cycle too long, and she'd faded. Everything about her was too pale—lips, complexion, eyes—even her eyebrows.

"Come on now, Hector, come on, I said—down." Eunice sounded like she was reading the words off a cue card. Hector totally ignored her, now running around to the driver's side of my truck, no doubt eager to make both sides match.

"Down, Hector. I said, down," Eunice repeated, this time with all the naked power in her voice of a limp dishrag. The dog was now digging at my door, its claws like tiny jackhammers.

"Oh, for crying out loud!" A huge shadow appeared behind Eunice's slight form. From where I sat in the truck, the only impression I got was massiveness. This mass aimed an enormous foot in Hector's direction, bellowing, "Hector, *no!*"

If that foot had connected, Hector might have been barking soprano from then on. The dog, however, saw the foot coming. Hector turned in a split second, gave one final growl in my direction, and disappeared around the side of the house, his tail between his legs.

Eunice and the mass beside her stood there for a

second, watching me in silence as I got out of my truck. "Sorry about that," the mass said. He didn't sound sorry.

The mass had to be Joe Eddy. Older, of course, but definitely Joe Eddy Krebbs. Standing there next to his thin wife, he was the human equivalent of an eclipse. One move, and Joe Eddy could easily block out the sun. It didn't seem possible, but I was sure he was even bigger than I remembered him being in high school. At least 6 feet, 5 inches, he had to weigh over 300 pounds. Joe Eddy looked as if he might have a strong influence on the tides.

Eunice, on the other hand, would have had to work hard to cast a shadow. She couldn't have been any more than 5 feet, 2 inches, and if she weighed 100 pounds, it could only have been because her clothes were heavy. I looked at the two of them, and wondered if Joe Eddy had been stealing Eunice's food.

I smiled at them both, and said, "Howdy, folks. I'm Haskell Blevins. I called earlier? I don't know if you all remember me, but I went to high school with you two." Both Eunice and Joe Eddy stared at me blankly.

"Yeah?" Joe Eddy said.

So much for the old school spirit.

"You all were a couple of years behind me," I went on, still smiling. "But I sure remember you two, all right." My voice was unnaturally cheery. As I spoke, I glanced real nonchalant over at the side of my truck. Sure enough, around the doorhandle were several nasty scratches. My smile froze.

Joe Eddy's eyes followed mine. Clearing his throat, he said, "Bad thing about coming down these here country roads. Your truck can get pretty beat up. Going by all them branches hanging in the road."

So that was how he was going to play it, was he? I opened my mouth to ask Joe Eddy if he'd ever seen a tree branch covered in brown fur, and I noticed Joe Eddy start to frown. It was like watching a tornado form.

I am barely 6 feet, and I tip the scales at 180 after a big meal. It didn't take an Einstein to figure out who was going to win any argument between Joe Eddy and me. Joe Eddy could have somebody like me for breakfast. And, judging from the looks of him, he probably had.

Sanity prevailed. I closed my mouth.

I was beginning to hope old Joe Eddy here really had done something awful to his wife's grandmother. I would enjoy putting him behind bars.

We moved on into the house, while I mentally calculated whether it would cost more than the $100 deductible I carried on my car insurance to get those scratches painted out.

"So what is it you wanted to talk to us about?" The couch groaned as Joe Eddy sat down. "I don't imagine you've come all the way out here just to talk about how we went to high school together." Joe Eddy grunted and added, "If'n you're selling something, you're a-wasting your time."

I glanced over at Eunice. She'd settled herself into a big overstuffed chair right by the door, and was now looking at her hands, folded primly in her lap. Her face was as pale as death.

Apparently, the woman hadn't told Joe Eddy a word about my impending visit. I cleared my throat, taking the straight-backed wooden chair next to the couch. It was about as comfortable as being perched on a sawhorse. "Well, Joe Eddy," I said, "I've been asked by your sister-in-law, Cordelia, to investigate the unfortunate death of Mrs. Turley—''

Joe Eddy didn't let me finish. "Oh, yeah?" he said. "Now, why would Cordelia have you questioning *us?* Huh? Answer me *that.*"

I gave him a calm smile. "Just to get more information about that night. That's all." I looked over at Eunice and gave her a smile, too. "Cordelia told me you two were particularly fond of Mrs. Turley—and that you'd be glad to help me any way you could."

That appeal seemed to have no affect at all on Joe Eddy. He grimaced, and squirmed as much as he could, considering that he was sitting down. Eunice, however, looked stricken. "Oh, yes, of course," she said. "We both just adored Grammy. We miss her so much."

Joe Eddy looked bored. That "we" of Eunice's must have been a slight exaggeration.

"The only reason we moved out here was to keep an eye on Grammy and Grampap," Eunice went on.

"Oh?" I said.

"Why, yes, Grammy and Grampap was all by themselves out here, and when their next door neighbor put her house up for sale a year ago, why, I told Joe Eddy, we got to move out there. On account of Grammy needing more help here lately."

Joe Eddy roused himself to nod. "Grammy's train had slipped the tracks," he said.

A spark flashed in Eunice's eyes when he said that.

"Pardon?" I said, looking from one of them to the other.

"Grammy was off her trolley," Joe Eddy said. "Bonkers. Coo-coo. Nuts." Joe Eddy was a master of discretion.

Eunice looked back down at her lap, two red spots

19

of color appearing on each cheek. "Grammy was a little confused some of the time. That's all. She was just showing her age." Eunice's voice was very low—almost as if she were talking to herself—but evidently, Joe Eddy caught every word.

"You a-contradicting me?" he asked, glaring at Eunice.

She blinked once, and then gave a quick shake of her head. "No, Joe Eddy, 'course not." Her eyes began to swim with unshed tears.

Joe Eddy interrupted her with an impatient sigh. "Eunice, why don't you go on out to the kitchen, and get me and, uh, Haskell here some lemonade? Or tea? Or something?"

Eunice got up out of that chair just as if she were spring-loaded. "Sure, Joe Eddy," she said, not looking at either one of us, "I'd be glad to. I—I'll be right back." Just before she went out the door, she gave me a worried look over her shoulder.

Once Eunice was gone, Joe Eddy leaned forward. The couch groaned as if in agony this time. "I am a-telling you the truth—Grammy was a real nut case."

"What made you think that?" I asked. If he started telling me about how she wore her clothes backwards again, I was not going to be impressed.

"She'd be talking to you one minute, and the next she didn't have the foggiest idea what she'd been saying." Joe Eddy raised his eyebrows, as if to say, See?

I guess I didn't look convinced, because he went on, looking a little annoyed, "And she kept talking about people who were dead. Like she'd seen 'em just last week."

Now he was getting somewhere. "Who were these dead people she talked about?"

"Oh, let me see." Joe Eddy rubbed his chin while he thought. For Joe Eddy, thinking looked like quite an effort. "Ray Don Peters, for one. He was an old geezer that died about five months before Grammy. And then there was, uh, Myrldean Bleemel. She's been dead almost two years now."

I wanted to get this straight. "And Grammy still acted as if they were alive?"

Joe Eddy nodded his huge head. "Talked about them as if she'd seen them last week, or something. And she even said bad stuff about them."

I shook my head. "No kidding," I said. "Bad stuff, you say." I decided that on a IQ test, Joe Eddy would rank right up there with the third-graders.

"Complained about Myrldean not liking her cooking. Called Ray Don an asshole." Joe Eddy nodded his head again as if that said it all.

I nodded mine. "Grammy does sound a tad senile," I allowed. "Do you think this had anything at all to do with her death?"

Joe Eddy shrugged and looked blank for about a minute. It was as if his picture tube had burned out for a little while. "Uh, well," he finally said, "maybe it could be that Grammy hit *herself* on the head. I mean, uh, maybe she wasn't thinking real straight, and she fell and hit her head. Maybe it was just an accident."

The newspaper accounts I'd read had been pretty clear on this. Mrs. Turley had been hit at least twice on the back of the head. Did Joe Eddy expect me to believe that the woman had fallen, then gotten up and fallen *again?* Or was this obviously prominent member of the Pigeon Fork intelligentsia trying to convince me that the old lady had picked up something heavy and whacked herself twice with it?

21

I just looked at him. "Well, now, there's a thought," I said. I resisted the impulse to add that it was not just any ordinary thought, it was a thought that was unbelievably stupid. I didn't say that, though. I just smiled wider at Joe Eddy. "I'll have to look into that. But, before I do, I guess I need to know exactly what went on that Friday night."

Joe Eddy's eyes narrowed. "What do you mean?"

I couldn't decide whether Joe Eddy was so dumb he had trouble following a simple conversation—or if he was really trying to hide something. "What I mean is I need to know exactly what went on that Friday night." I spoke slowly and enunciated every word.

Joe Eddy said, "Oh." His picture tube burned out again for a couple of seconds, and then he said, "We were playing Rook."

Rook is what folks play around here instead of poker. It's a card game I think every resident of Pigeon Fork learns as soon as he's toilet trained. Maybe before. Rook is a lot like bridge, I guess, in that you make bids and you take tricks and you get real mad when you lose. And it's a lot like poker in that you can bet on each hand, you can lose your paycheck, and you can get really, really mad when you lose.

"Rook, you say," I said. I waited. Joe Eddy evidently was not about to say anything more until I asked. "And who all was here?"

Joe Eddy moved around again. The couch whimpered this time. "Well, uh, it was me and Grampap Turley and Delbert Sims."

I knew Delbert Sims. Well, I didn't exactly know him personally, but I knew of him. I wasn't sure what old Delbert did for a living, but I knew what he did for fun. He drank. I guess Delbert Sims would've been Pigeon Fork's town drunk, except that there were quite a few people vying for the position. From what I'd heard, though, I reckon Delbert was a frontrunner.

"Have you known Delbert Sims long?" I asked.

"As long as I been married to Eunice, and we got hitched right outta high school. He was a friend of the family. Fact is, I think he was engaged to Grammy once upon a time. Back when they was both in their twenties, I think. 'Course, Grammy was a few years older than Delbert.''

I made a mental note. Maybe old Delbert was still carrying around a grudge. Maybe he was still heart-broken over getting a "Dear Delbert" letter forty years ago. Stranger things have happened.

"So all of you were together the whole night?"

Joe Eddy nodded. "Even Grammy was here at first. She come over with Grampap about seven, stayed awhile jawing out in the kitchen with Eunice. What those two ever found to talk about was beyond me, but they could jaw for hours." He rolled his eyes. "Hours."

I tried to look sympathetic. Lord, how could the poor man stand it? His wife actually talking with her own grandmother. Often. What a cross this guy had to bear. Up until recently, of course. "Do you know what time Grammy left?"

"We'd played a couple of games by then. Musta been around nine. Maybe." He cocked his massive head at me, and winked. "That's what I told the law, anyway."

I didn't know if I should wink back or not. I decided against it. My luck, Joe Eddy would decide I was flirting with him.

"After Grammy left, then where was Eunice?"

Joe Eddy shrugged. "Right here in this room. She was over there crocheting on one of them afghans she's always making."

"And none of you ever left the room?"

Joe Eddy's eyes started looking like slits. Evidently, even a third-grader could figure out the direction I was heading. "So what if I did leave?" he said.

I smiled at him. "So nothing."

Joe Eddy didn't smile back. Instead, he leaned forward, menacingly. I could've sworn the house tilted a little. "Uh, look, I left the room to get me a Coke. That's all. And when I got to the kitchen, I just decided I better not. Being as how they got so much sugar in them and all."

I nodded. Joe Eddy looked like a man who was watching his weight. Lord, we all were.

"That asshole Sheriff Minrath in town tried to make something outta that," he grumbled. "Tried to make it into something awful. My not coming back with a Coke." He shook his head. "Can you believe that?"

Actually, I could. I knew Vergil Minrath pretty well. He'd gone to high school with my dad, and Vergil and I had worked real close on the Great Feedsack Caper that I mentioned earlier. Vergil was OK. He'd probably felt the same rush of warmth toward Joe Eddy that I was feeling myself.

I made another mental note—to go by Vergil's office real soon—even as I was shaking my head sympathetically in Joe Eddy's direction. "Well, now, that's the law for you," I said. "Always jumping to ridiculous conclusions." This time I leaned forward. The chair I was sitting in made no sound at all. "Tell me, did anyone else leave during that night?"

Joe Eddy brightened. I'd evidently asked the right question. "Of course, they did. *Everybody* left at one

time or t'other," he said. "Delbert left for his beer.
He kept a cooler of it out in the trunk of his car." Joe
Eddy smirked. "Between you and me, I think old
Delbert was too lazy to carry the thing in here—so he
just kept leaving to get more."

"He left more than once?" I asked.

Joe Eddy smiled. Not a pretty sight. "More'n once.
And then, of course, there was Grampap. He left a lot
of times to take a leak."

Eunice came bustling in right then, carrying a tray
with two glasses with ice, and a pitcher of lemonade.
"How many times do you think Grampap left during
the card game that night?" Joe Eddy directed his
question at his wife.

Eunice actually jumped, the ice cubes in the lemonade pitcher ricocheting off the sides. "Oh. Well. Goodness," she said, putting the tray down on the coffee
table none too soon. Her eyes looked like a cornered rabbit, darting from one of us to the other.
"I—I guess maybe a couple?"

Joe Eddy looked annoyed. "Maybe a couple? Are
you kidding? At least, uh, five times, I'd say." He
turned to me. "Beer always was real hard on the old
man's kidneys."

"He—he wasn't gone long," Eunice put in, her
voice shaking.

"None of us was gone long," Joe Eddy said. "Eunice here went up to bed about eleven-thirty, and we
played another couple of hours maybe. Like we always did."

"They been playing Rook on Friday nights for years
now," Eunice said. She stopped, and looked away.
" 'Course now—" She broke off, blinking back tears.
For a second, I could see the family resemblance to
Cordelia.

Joe Eddy shrugged. "Grampap ain't much interested in Rook no more." There was disapproval in
his tone. As if quitting playing cards on account of a
little thing like having your wife murdered was carrying things a bit far. Joe Eddy was one empathetic
soul.

I sat there, watching Eunice pouring the lemonade
into our glasses. Her face was flushed a little now,
her eyes glistening with unshed tears, and for a fleeting moment I could see plain as day the shy, pretty
girl she'd been back in high school. The girl I remembered. She might even be pretty again, if she washed
her hair real good, gained some weight, and wore
something else besides that faded loose housedress
and those pink terry cloth bedroom slippers.

Makeup might help, too. And telling Joe Eddy to
find himself another doormat.

I thanked Eunice for the lemonade, and she looked
surprised. Like maybe she hadn't been thanked for
anything in the last ten, fifteen years. "Tell me
about Grammy," I said.

Eunice actually smiled this time. It made me even
more convinced that she was still a pretty girl. A
pretty girl hiding inside an ugly woman's housedress.
"Oh, Grammy was wonderful," she said, sitting herself down in the overstuffed chair again. "She was
more like my mama than my grandmama. She raised
me and Cordelia, you know, ever since our parents
got killed in a car wreck. I was only six when it
happened. And Cordelia had only just turned four.
Grammy was already in her forties, but she took us
in, anyway."

Eunice paused for breath, her eyes moist. "Grammy
was the sweetest thing. She loved flowers, you know.
She had the prettiest garden. Every year it was differ-

ent. One year she'd have marigolds and petunias, and the next—"

Joe Eddy held up his hand. "Okay, okay, Eunice," he said, "we already know Grammy was a saint."

Eunice clamped her mouth shut just as if she'd been slapped. I made up my mind right then I'd try to talk to Eunice about Grammy one day when Joe Eddy wasn't around. If that ever happened. It looked as if he kept her on a pretty tight rein.

"Was there anyone you know of who might have wished your grandmother harm?" I asked. "Or someone who might have particularly disliked her pets?"

Joe Eddy and Eunice exchanged a glance, and then shook their heads in unison. "Everybody we know liked Grammy," Joe Eddy said.

"Everybody," Eunice echoed.

"And most everybody didn't care one way or the other about her pets," Joe Eddy added. " 'Course, that cat was a pain. That damn Percival would scratch your eyes out if you gave him half a chance."

Eunice turned even paler. "He's dead," she said real low. She'd set the pitcher down, and was looking at her lap again. Her point, apparently, was that you don't speak badly of the dead, even if the dead is a cat.

Joe Eddy gave her a look. "I know he's dead. Didn't I bury that dumb cat? *And* that stupid bird?"

Eunice winced.

Joe Eddy turned back to me. "Would you believe that Emmaline Johnston wanted us to have a funeral for the pets? The day after burying Grammy?" Joe Eddy threw back his head and hooted. For a man his size, he had a high, almost girlish laugh. "Like a double feature or something!"

I smiled politely. Poor Eunice did not. "Emmaline Johnston?" I repeated. The name sounded familiar.

Joe Eddy wiped his eyes, and said, "Damn fool woman's with the Ladies' Auxiliary. She's been writing letters to the editor and anybody else she can think of."

I remembered then. Emmaline Johnston's name should be familiar to me. I'd seen it often enough in print. As I recalled, she owned something like nine or ten cats herself. The death of Grammy's cat, Percival, had hit her hard. Emmaline Johnston must've had a letter to the editor in every edition of the *Pigeon Fork Gazette* since the murder. Her letters dwelt heavily on finding "the monster who'd done this to this poor defenseless animal." I'm fairly certain Emmaline's last letter didn't even mention Mrs. Turley.

Joe Eddy was starting to shuffle his feet a little, tapping his huge shoe against the gleaming surface of the coffee table. It was getting time for me to be on my way, each shoe tap said. "I guess you all didn't hear anything unusual that night?" I asked.

"Nope," Joe Eddy said. The shoe taps got louder.

I tried not to look at Joe Eddy's shoes. "Well, I guess I need to know just one more thing," I said. "Whereabouts does Delbert Sims live?"

The shoe taps abruptly stopped. "Now, what would you want to know that for?" Joe Eddy asked, his eyes like slits.

I shrugged, real casual. "I reckon I better talk to Delbert, too. Cordelia would want me to."

Joe Eddy stared at me. When I'd given up on him ever making another sound, he finally said, "Delbert's in the phone book."

That appeared to be all I was going to get out of Joe Eddy.

I stood up. "Well, thanks a lot for your help," I said. I mean, suggesting that I look up somebody's address in the phone book—what an original idea. I wish I'd thought of it.

I turned to Eunice. "And I sure do appreciate your help—" Joe Eddy had gotten to his feet right after I did. He started moving toward the door, herding me along in front of him. It was like having a tidal wave gaining on you. I quit talking and quickened my pace.

At the door, however, I stopped. I would've kept on going, except that Hector was on the other side of the screen. At the sight of me, the dog began jumping at the screen, doing a canine imitation of a homicidal maniac. It was convincing. The bared teeth and the snarl were nice touches.

Joe Eddy looked over at Hector and then back at me. "Uh, you want me to tie him up?"

No, Joe Eddy, I want Hector to grab me by the leg and drag me around your yard by it. That's what I thought. What I said was, "I'd sure appreciate it. I'll be going over next door to talk to Grampap if he's home, so I'd like you to keep your dog tied up for a while, okay?"

Joe Eddy's eyes were wary again. He glanced over at the Pepto Bismol house speculatively. "Sure, no problem," he said. He stepped out the door, and grabbed the dog's collar, hauling the little maniac toward a rusty chain attached to a large tree in the side yard.

When Joe Eddy went out the door, I turned to Eunice. "By the way," I said, "have you ever heard of somebody named Ray Don Peters or Myrldean Bleemel?"

Eunice's reaction surprised me. She gave a little start. Like maybe a bee had just stung her. She recovered right away, though, running a shaky hand through her limp hair. "Ray Don and Myrldean used to be friends of Grammy's," she said. Even her mouth suddenly looked pale. "They passed away, though, some time ago." She paused here and tried to sound casual. "Why do you ask?"

I shrugged. "Oh, just curious," I said.

Hector was chained up by then. I opened the screen door, and gave Eunice a smile. "Well, thanks again."

She gave me a smile in return. Her smile, however, did little to hide the fear in her eyes.

I went out that door, thinking that either one of two things was true. Either Eunice was in a perpetual state of scared—which you could understand, being as how she had to look at Joe Eddy across the breakfast table every single day—or else, she knew more than she was telling. A lot more.

CHAPTER
THREE

I got into my truck and drove it into the gravel driveway of the Pepto Bismol house next door to Joe Eddy's. My thinking was that it would be nice to have the truck within running distance of Grampap's door in case the rusty chain around Hector's neck happened to break.

All the time I was pulling into the driveway, Joe Eddy stood out in his side yard and watched. What he found so all-fired interesting was beyond me. I guess maybe he just wanted to remind me that he was there.

He needn't have bothered. Trying to ignore Joe Eddy would've been like trying to ignore Mount Rushmore.

I got out of my truck and walked on up to the front door. Up close, the Pepto Bismol pink was even more nauseating than it was at a distance. Joe Eddy was, of course, still standing there in his yard, so I looked back over at him and waved. Real friendlylike.

Joe Eddy didn't wave back. Real unfriendlylike.

The dog at Joe Eddy's feet, however, did everything but wave. The minute I moved, he went through
his maniac routine. Lunging, snarling, barking, clawing
—the whole bit. Evidently, Hector did not see any
difference at all between his own yard and that of
Grampap's. Hector was determined to have a nervous breakdown if anybody set foot in either one.

By the time I got to the front porch, the dog had
stretched his chain full length and, in his delirium,
was trying his best to wrap the chain around Joe
Eddy's legs.

"Holy shit!" Joe Eddy yelled, trying to dodge the
chain. "Stop it, Hector, *stop,* you son of a bitch!"
Which, if you think about it, is not exactly an insult
to a dog. I decided not to point this out to Joe Eddy.
He seemed to have enough to think about as it was.

The front door was standing wide open, and I could
see through the screen door right into the living room.
The curtains were pulled, so there wasn't a whole lot
of light in there, but I could make out an old man,
sitting on a couch against the opposite wall. He was
wearing a plaid workshirt, faded overalls, and no
shoes. He was also wearing a real big grin on his face.

I could see right away what was making him so
cheerful. He was watching a large color TV which, as
best as I could tell, was tuned to one of them triple-X
rated channels. On the screen several amply endowed,
naked ladies were rolling around in the mud, trying
not to get so covered in the stuff you couldn't see
how amply endowed they were.

Grampap, Lord love him, was my kind of guy.

I knocked on the door.

Grampap jumped as if he'd been shot. He grabbed
a remote control and snapped off the TV.

"Who's there?" he asked, getting up and shuffling

toward the door. He didn't sound at all cheerful anymore.

I told him who I was and what I was there for. He actually looked relieved as he held open the door for me. "I was afraid you were from church," he said with a sheepish smile. "The pastor and some of the deacons from my church have been looking in on me every week or so ever since—since—"

His voice sort of trailed off, so I jumped in real quick and changed the subject. "I didn't know you could get cable all the way out here," I said, sitting down in a chair covered in pink floral chintz. A crocheted doily lay across the back and in the middle of each side arm.

"You can't," Grampap said, settling himself back down on the couch. It was bright pink, and it had the same assortment of doilies as my chair. Grampap pointed toward the back of the house. "I got me a satellite dish a couple of weeks ago. You can see it if you walk around back." He smiled happily. "Yep, got me a dish. Always wanted one." He stopped then, looking over at me, as if maybe he'd already said too much.

I gave him a smile that was meant to be reassuring.

The old man, however, didn't look any too reassured. He rubbed his stubbled chin and said, "Now, look, young feller, I sure don't want you a-thinking I'm glad all this happened. I miss that woman. I surely do." He glanced toward a large framed portrait prominently displayed on top of the TV, and his eyes misted up. "We were married almost fifty years. That's a long time."

He's telling me? I was married once myself—and it was the longest four years of my life. I can't imagine being married to anybody for fifty years—and if that anybody just happened to be my ex-wife, I can't imagine either one of us actually surviving for fifty years. Not without weapons, anyway.

I glanced over at the portrait Grampap was looking at, and I almost did a double-take. This was Grammy? The picture showed a large, big-boned woman with piercing blue eyes and a long, straight nose. She had pale skin just like her granddaughters, but in the portrait she was wearing more makeup than the two of her granddaughters put together. Her hair was short and curly and—believe it or not—a bright orangey-red.

It was with some effort that I kept my mouth from dropping open. Grammy certainly didn't look like your typical grandmother. In fact, from where I sat, she didn't look a day over fifty-five.

Grampap was still going on. "I like to think Grammy would be real happy if she knew I'd gotten the dish. I know, if I'd been the first to go, I'd have been real happy if my life insurance had given Grammy something she'd always wanted."

I turned to smile at him again, tearing my eyes away from the portrait. I could've been wrong, but Grammy didn't look like the sort of woman who would be "real happy" to know her husband was spending his time grinning at naked ladies on TV.

So, the way I looked at it, Grampap Turley had given himself a pretty good motive for murder the minute I walked in the door. And yet, I was inclined to believe what he said about missing her. I know this sounds unprofessional, but Grampap sure didn't look like the murdering type. If, of course, there was such a thing.

He was about four inches shorter than me and a lot thinner. He must've been in his early seventies, but he still had a full head of hair. Unlike Grammy, though, his hair was snow white. He kept it brushed back from his face, so that it stood up around his ears like white wings.

His eyes were a clear china blue, and when he spoke, he looked directly at you. Unwavering. If he had killed his wife to get a satellite dish, he had real talent as an actor. Or absolutely no conscience at all.

I remembered then what Cordelia had told me about her not getting any insurance money as yet. "Then you've already gotten paid by the insurance company?" I asked.

Grampap nodded. "The insurance policy I had on Grammy was with Mutual Life. The company Grammy chose was Heritage Mutual." His blue eyes twinkled. "And she was always telling me she could do anything better'n me. Well, I guess I picked out the best insurance company, now didn't I?"

"I reckon you did," I said.

"Pshaw," he added, "I'd have told Grammy, too, which one she should've gone with. If'n she'd asked. But I didn't even know she was a-buying those policies for the grandkids. She just took the money out of the bank without even telling me." Grampap's tone was aggrieved. Those blue eyes were staring straight at me again. " 'Course she was forgetting a lot here lately. It mighta slipped her mind."

I nodded. "Cordelia told me she was a little absent-minded." Absent in the mind was probably more like it, but I didn't say that.

Evidently, though, even "absent-minded" wasn't a good enough euphemism. Grampap started looking irate. "Now I sure hope them young folks didn't give you the wrong idea about Grammy. She was just fine, she was."

I looked toward the portrait again. "She certainly was a fine-looking woman. Is that a recent photo?"

Grampap grinned. "Grammy always took pride in her looks. She was sixty-six when that picture was taken. Just a year ago. She gave me that picture for Christmas." He swiped at his eyes with the back of one gnarled hand, and looked away. "Grammy always was real thoughtful," he said in a choked voice.

There was a long, uncomfortable silence. I've mentioned how bad I am in situations like this, haven't I? Well, I'm even worse than I said. Finally, scrambling in my mind for something to say, I came up with, "You sure have a nice place here." Lord.

Grampap looked back over at me. "It is nice, ain't it?" he said, blinking rapidly. "I got me nine acres here, same as Joe Eddy and Eunice next door."

I was surprised that either of them had that much land. And relieved to be talking about something that didn't make the old man's eyes water. "Your property must run back into the woods," I said, by way of making conversation.

Grampap nodded. "Matter of fact, mine and Joe Eddy's property ends on the other side of the woods," he said. " 'Course, I don't get back there much. I'd rather just sit on my back porch, and look at the trees." His voice had gotten back to normal. Thank goodness.

"Well, I don't want to take up much of your time," I said. "I just talked to Eunice and Joe Eddy, and—"

Grampap interrupted me. "And, I reckon you'll be a-wanting to hear from me what happened that night." He sounded a little shaky again.

I nodded. Grampap sighed, and started in. He told his story real slow, stopping every so often to scratch his chin, but, for the most part, his account matched

Joe Eddy's real close. It almost matched too close. I found myself wondering if maybe Joe Eddy hadn't given Grampap a little help with his remembering.

Grampap did, however, remember one thing different. How many times Joe Eddy had left the living room that night. "I reckon Joe Eddy went into the kitchen a couple of times while we were playing," Grampap said.

"Was this before or after Grammy went on home?" I asked.

Grampap gave me a look before he answered. He knew what I was getting at.

"It was after," he said. "But that don't mean nothing. We all knew what Joe Eddy was doing out there in the kitchen."

"Getting a drink?" I put in.

Grampap shook his head. "Naw! Oh, that's what he said he was doing, but he never came back with one." He chuckled then. "Naw, he was in there trying to cool off some. Joe Eddy has got to be just about the poorest loser I ever did see. And he was losing bad that night." Grampap hooked his thumbs around his overall suspenders and leaned back against the couch. "So he kept going out to the kitchen, to keep from having a screaming fit right in front of us." He grinned and shook his white head. "Joe Eddy is one terrible Rook player." His grin faded as he added, "And he's got a real bad temper."

He seemed about to say more, but then he hushed up.

I hated to do it, but I had to hear the rest. "And then what happened?" I asked.

Grampap sighed again, and reached down to brush some nonexistent dirt off his overalls. "Well," he said. From the way he pronounced it, you would've thought the word was spelled w-e-l-p. There was a long pause, and then finally he said, "I reckon the game busted up about one-thirty. After that Delbert went home, and I went home and—and I found her." He got heavily to his feet. "Here, I'll show you."

We moved on out to the kitchen. In here there were white curtains trimmed in pink rickrack at the windows, and pink and white potholders on the stove. The white linoleum floor looked as if it had just been waxed. On the bookshelf next to the broom closet, cookbooks and catalogues were neatly arranged. I looked at Grampap in amazement. Did he keep this house this clean all by himself?

Grampap must've been reading my mind. "I ain't waxed yet today, so this kitchen is kind of a mess," he said. I looked around. What was he talking about? Everything looked spotless. Grampap's floor didn't just look like you could eat off it. You could have surgery on it. Without thinking twice.

Beside me Grampap took another deep breath and pointed to a spot on the floor next to the table. "She was lying right there. And right next to her was that poor cat. And a little ways off was that poor bird."

He drew yet another ragged breath. "Makes me feel bad for every bad thing I ever said."

I gave him a smile I hoped looked every bit as sympathetic as I was feeling. "That's natural," I said. "After something like this happens, you always do feel bad for anything you ever did to somebody—"

Grampap just looked at me like I was talking in a foreign language. "Oh, I wasn't talking about Grammy," he said. "I never said nothing bad about *her*. She'd have made me sorry I was ever *born*. Naw, I was talking about her cat and bird. I reckon I wasn't very nice to that cat, Percival. I had reason, though." He nodded his head emphatically. "I mean, that Percival would just as soon scratch you as look at you. Particularly those last weeks. And he was always after that bird—Lordy! Sweety-bird had a lot of close calls, I'm here to tell you—"

I stopped smiling. I was afraid if I smiled, I might go all the way into laughter.

Grampap had warmed to his subject by then, and he didn't need any encouragement anyway. "I reckon I complained about that bird some, too. It was always getting out of its cage, and flying around." He fixed me with a look. "Birds are dirty." He said it as if he were repeating a horrible fact.

I nodded. You can't argue with facts.

"It must be tough keeping this place up alone," I said. Trying to sound sympathetic again.

Grampap again looked at me in surprise. "Not really," he said, "I did all the cleaning before. Not to talk bad about her, but Grammy couldn't clean her way out of a paper bag."

Now, what do you say to that? I chose not to say anything.

Grampap didn't seem to notice. He was looking back over at the floor. "I had a terrible time cleaning them outlines off the linoleum. If Grammy knew how those police had marked up our floor, she'd have been so mad," Grampap said.

I glanced over at him. He was serious.

"I guess the police just don't think of those things," I said weakly.

Grampap went on as if I hadn't even spoken. His eyes were far away by then. "From what I could gather, Grammy was a-sitting right there," he said, pointing at the kitchen table, "planning her garden, like she does every year, and somebody musta come up behind her." Grampap looked away, blinking fast. I couldn't stand to watch, so I moved over to the table.

On top of the table were a couple of pencils and a notebook pad. I looked at the pad, and then looked quickly back at Grampap. He was noisily clearing his throat.

On the pad, amazingly enough, was a sketch of a flower garden. Sections of the penciled rectangle had been labeled "snapdragons," "periwinkles," "petunias," "marigolds," and several other flowers I'd never even heard of. On the side of the paper beside the sketch was a list. Name of flower, how many seed packets, price per packet, and a total. Next to the pad were two pencils and an outdated seed catalogue. "Is this—?" I started to ask, but Grampap answered me before I even finished.

"I ain't touched a thing on that table," he said, holding up his hand as if he expected to be scolded. "I've left everything just the way she had it that night."

I was studying the list. Petunias, 3 packets, $1.25 per packet, $3.75 total. Snapdragons, 4 packets, $1.15 per packet, $4.60 total. Grammy must've been a stickler for detail. The entry after "Marigolds" had been carefully erased. I couldn't tell what it had been, but it now read 3 packets, $1.25 per packet, $3.75 total. The list went on and on, in a small, neat script. With erasures here and there. Like maybe Grammy had changed her mind or something.

Grampap was watching me by then, his eyes sad. "She got her new seed catalogue in the mail the very next day." He shuffled over to the bookshelf and showed me a thick book with "Harvee's Seed" in big green letters on the front. "Grammy was always so tickled to get her new one," Grampap said wistfully.

If the grief in the old man's eyes was not the real thing, he sure had me fooled. "You know," I said gently, "you don't have to keep this here anymore. The police will have photographs—"

Grampap shook his head emphatically. "Oh, no. Grammy would kill me if I messed with her stuff."

The second he said that, it was just like a cold wind blew through the room. I actually felt like shivering. Talk about not knowing what to say. Finally, I managed, "Well, now, she'd probably understand—"

Grampap shook his white head again. "You don't know her! One time I came home with some house paint—a nice ivory color—on account of I was fed up with looking at that pink." He ran his hand through his hair. When he was finished, it looked even more like white wings were coming out of his ears. "—and Grammy had herself a fit! Made me take that paint right back to the store. Without even opening it!"

I was starting to think that maybe it wasn't just Grammy's trolley that had slipped the tracks. Maybe going nuts had been a group effort. And yet, how crazy could Grampap be if he hated that pink?

" 'Course now, with her gone, I can't ever paint the house," Grampap said, his eyes agitated. "She'd be furious!"

I decided right then that even crazy people could have good taste in exterior finishes. I took a step away from him. "But, Mr. Turley, surely you realize that—"

He interrupted me. "You don't understand. Pink was her favorite color," he said. As if that explained everything.

I just looked at him. He must've known what I was thinking, though, because he calmed down right away. Even chuckled a little. Looking straight at me with those clear blue eyes. "I guess I sound nuts, don't I?"

He had me there.

"Well, young fella, if'n you were my age, you'd understand. I'm seventy-two and I am going to be meeting up with Grammy again real soon. I'd sure hate to spend eternity with her if she's in a bad mood."

He had a point there. I wondered if he thought Grammy approved of what he was watching on television these days, but I didn't say anything. My eyes, though, kind of flickered back toward the living room.

Grampap grinned. The old man could've gotten work as a mind reader. "Oh, Grammy wouldn't care if I was watching other women on TV—naw, it's only if I actually went out with another woman that she'd kill me." The old man beamed at me. "Grammy always said I could window-shop all I wanted, as long as I never tried to buy anything!"

For a lady who was dead, Grammy still exerted a real powerful influence.

Grampap started shuffling on back into the living room, and I followed him. When we were sitting down again where I could get a good look at his face, I said, "I wanted to ask you one more thing. Have you ever heard of some people named Ray Don Peters or Myrldean Bleemel?"

Unlike Eunice, Grampap didn't look at all alarmed. He just nodded his head. "Yep, those were friends of my Grammy's. Dead now, though."

"Oh?" I said. Looking dumb. I do that real well on occasion. Particularly when I'm talking to somebody who is still taking his orders from a dead woman.

"Myrldean and Grammy went to school together.

42

They was real close. Grammy cried her eyes out when Myrldean died about two years ago. Fell down the steps, as I recollect."

"Did Grammy ever talk about Myrldean?"

Grampap looked away before he spoke. For the first time, I had the feeling he was lying. "Oh, she talked about her some." His voice was evasive. "About how much she missed her, things like that."

"And Mr. Peters?"

Grampap made a short, scornful sound. "He weren't no *Mr.* Peters. He was just an old fool. Thought he was some kind of ladies' man." Grampap made yet another one of those scornful sounds.

"How did he die?"

Grampap shrugged. "Nobody really knows for sure. He was found in his basement with a bump on his head. 'Bout a year ago. Folks reckoned he just up and fell."

Grampap did not sound at all unhappy that Ray Don Peters had departed this earth. I made another mental note. Maybe Ray Don's family might have more to say on the subject. Who knows? Maybe the deaths of Grammy and Ray Don—and maybe even Myrldean—were related in some way. Although this wouldn't account for Grammy's pets. How would you explain them?

"Did Grammy ever talk about Ray Don?"

Grampap looked at a spot on his overalls. "Can't say that she did," he said. "They weren't all that gooda friends."

I was pretty sure he was lying again, but why? It sure didn't make any sense that I could see.

I'd run out of questions. I shook Grampap's hand, thanked him for his help, and started to move toward the door.

Grampap followed me. "I sure hope you find who did this. The police ain't been much help—" He swiped at his eyes again. "Grammy was a fine woman. She had a lot of class. She sure don't deserve to go this way—and have her killer get off scot-free."

I looked over at him. There was real fury in the old man's eyes. "I'll do what I can," I promised.

As soon as we got close to the door, Hector must've heard us. I could hear him out there, revving up into a full-scale fit. "One other thing—" I said, stepping out onto the pink front porch. "—was the dog next door out that night?"

The old man nodded, his eyes on mine.

"Do you remember if it barked?"

Grampap stopped still. "Why, now that you mention it, Hector didn't bark once." He scratched his chin. "Now, ain't that funny?"

Funny is not the word I would've used.

CHAPTER

FOUR

It took me thirty minutes to get back to my office. Thirty minutes of eating more dirt, and bouncing over more potholes. Once I was finally back, it took me another five minutes or so to actually get around to climbing the stairs up to my office. This was on account of Melba running out of Elmo's Drugstore and flagging me down the minute I stepped out of my truck.

"So, what's the verdict, Haskell?" Melba said, her hands on each meaty hip. "Are we taking the case or not?"

I just stared at her. It was the "we" in that sentence that bothered me. My phone rings down at the drugstore, too, so that when I'm out, Melba can take my messages. I even pay part of Melba's salary so she'll actually answer the phone for me instead of just sitting there and letting it ring, the way she does Elmo's phone.

The only trouble is, ever since I put Melba on my payroll, she seems to think we're in business together. It's like she wants to play Della Street to my Perry Mason. I took a deep breath before I answered. "As a matter of fact, *I* am taking the case."

This subtlety was lost on Melba. Her round face brightened. "Then you really think we can find out who wasted the old lady and the livestock?"

When Melba is doing her Della Street impression, she starts talking like every hard-boiled detective she's ever seen on TV. It's a little scary.

It's also scary how fast word travels in this town. Cordelia had probably mentioned in passing to somebody or another that I was working for her, and that was all that it took.

Or maybe Melba herself had cornered Cordelia as she was leaving my office. I wouldn't put it past Melba to hold somebody hostage until they blabbed. Melba thinks it's the world's duty to keep her informed.

I took another deep breath. "Well, Melba, *I* can't say for sure *I'm* going to solve this thing, but *I* sure can say *I'm* going to do my best." This time, for good measure, I put a little extra emphasis on every one of the I's. I turned and started up to my office.

Undaunted, Melba followed right behind me, huffing and puffing her way up the stairs. When she finally came through my office door, she just stood there for a long moment, getting her wind back. Then she walked straight over and sat herself down on a corner of my desk.

I went and sat down in my chair, trying not to look as annoyed as I felt. For one thing, I don't want to make Melba mad, or my chances of ever getting my phone answered again are slim to none. For another thing, Melba *is* the sole support of five children, so I really shouldn't wish her bodily harm.

"So, tell me, Chief," Melba said, crossing her plump legs, "what's our next move?"

I hate it when she calls me Chief, but I decided to let that one pass. "Melba," I said quietly, "*your* next move is to get back downstairs before Elmo notices you're gone."

Melba pouted, swinging one chubby foot in a small circle. I noticed then that she was sitting smack-dab on top of yesterday's mail. I got myself a free sample in the mail yesterday, too. Hand lotion in one of them little aluminum squares that you're supposed to tear open. No doubt flattened by now, and oozing all over. I forced myself not to look in that direction.

"Then I guess you don't want to know the latest on Eunice and Joe Eddy?" Melba's foot stopped swinging as she looked over at me, a small smile playing around her pink-tinted mouth.

I didn't smile back, because now it looked like Melba even knew who I'd just gone and talked to, for God's sake. I mean, Lord, why did anybody even bother publishing a newspaper in this town? Why didn't they just tell Melba?

But I know when I'm licked. "All right, all right," I said, sighing, "what about Eunice and Joe Eddy?"

Melba looked like a light bulb had just gone on behind her small blue eyes. She leaned toward me and said, "Well, talk is that the Krebbses aren't happy."

I stared at her. *This* was news? If Melba had found somebody who *would* be happy living with Joe Eddy, *that* would be news.

Melba must've known what I was thinking, because she held up her hand. Her fingers looked like small sausages. "Talk is," Melba said, "Joe Eddy might even be smacking Eunice around." Melba lifted one penciled eyebrow and nodded emphatically. "Oh, yeah, that's what they say. That Joe Eddy is one mean son of a gun."

This might've been what Grampap had been hinting at when he told me that Joe Eddy had a real bad temper. I didn't want to believe it. Poor Eunice. "Has anybody ever actually *seen* Joe Eddy hit Eunice?"

Melba shrugged. "You don't think he'd be dumb enough to smack her around in public, do you?"

Remembering Joe Eddy, of course, I did. But I didn't say it. What I said was, "If this is true, then why on earth would Eunice stay with him?"

Melba shrugged. "Maybe Eunice is afraid to leave. And, then again, I heard tell they got themselves hitched right outta high school, just like me and Otis. Maybe Joe Eddy is a hard habit for Eunice to break." Melba looked away, her small eyes suddenly getting misty. "When you've been high-school sweethearts all your life, it's real hard to let go, you know."

I swallowed, feeling uncomfortable. From what I'd heard, Melba and her husband Otis and the entire Hawley brood had only been in Pigeon Fork a few months when Otis had his heart attack. That had been a little over two years ago. The Hawleys had evidently just moved here from an even smaller small town—Indian Knee, Kentucky. The youngest Hawley had been less than a year old when Otis died. It had to be rough on poor Melba, suddenly having to raise five kids alone.

Melba now blinked a couple of times and patted distractedly at her beehive. "Yeah, it's always tough to say goodbye to your first real love," she said, her voice a little hoarse. I'd never met Otis, but Melba had shown me his picture once. I remembered his beefy, pockmarked face. I had to hand it to Melba. Anybody who could look at *that* face—and still talk about "real love"—was quite a woman.

Melba cleared her throat, and started swinging her foot again. "Of course, it don't help any that Eunice is such a mouse. I mean, really," she said, rolling her eyes. She then leaned toward me, pointing a sausage-finger at my nose. "I tell you one thing, if a man ever laid a hand on *me,* he'd sure be sorry!"

Looking at Melba, I didn't doubt it for a minute. Between Joe Eddy and Melba, though, it might be close to a fair fight. But between Joe Eddy and Eunice?

Melba's eyes were eager now. "So, Chief, do you think that—on account of Joe Eddy having such a violent nature—that it's probably him that's the perp?"

This is another thing Melba has got from watching detectives on television. Calling a suspect the perp, short for perpetrator. I try to keep my face real still as I answer, so I don't laugh right in Melba's face. "Actually, I think it's too early to say, Melba. I mean, we don't even know for sure that Joe Eddy—"

From downstairs came the unmistakable sound of Elmo in full rage. "Melba!" he yelled. *"Melba! Melllllba!"*

Melba bounced down from the edge of my desk. "Well, I can't be sitting around, jawing up here. I best get back to work," she said, patting at her bee-hive again and smoothing her skirt. "I'm betting on Joe Eddy, though. You mark my words," she said. "But I'll be giving it some more thought, okay? And I'll be right downstairs if you need to talk."

I watched Melba head toward the door. I needed to talk to her, all right. One of these days. In fact, it looked like I had to have a long, long talk with Melba.

It's one thing to feel a little sorry for her having all them kids to raise and all, but that doesn't mean I've got to take the woman on as a partner. Della Street, she ain't.

Melba stopped dead in the doorway, looking back toward me over her shoulder. "Oh, by the way," she said, "some woman's been calling you all morning."

I waited, but Melba had apparently said all she intended to.

Melba's messages are almost always like this one. "Some woman." "Some man." "A guy." Sometimes, I almost wish she wouldn't even tell me. Other times, I suspect she's doing this on purpose, just to torture me.

"Did whoever it was leave a number?" I asked. My tone was real patient, even though I was pretty certain I already knew the answer.

Sure enough, Melba gave me one of her looks. "Not really," she said. I knew what that meant. Whoever it was had tried to leave a number, but with Melba it was hopeless.

Melba blinked a couple of times, real innocent. "Anyway, I *told* her you'd be back," she said. "Soon."

I took another deep breath. I think I was getting ready to start hyperventilating by then. "Melba, do you suppose you could get a name and a number next time? I think I've mentioned this before," I said.

Actually, I *knew* I'd mentioned it before. Time and time again. Apparently Melba interprets "answering the phone" real literally. She thinks that just picking it up is all that's required.

Melba was beginning to look irritated now. She rolled her eyes at me and turned back toward the stairs. As always, she was muttering to herself. Something about "try to do a guy a favor—"

I watched Melba waddling away and wondered. Do you suppose Perry ever felt like slapping Della silly?

I might as well admit that it gave me a small satisfaction to see the damp smudge of lotion on Melba's backside as she moved away from me. I decided not to mention it to her. Let it be a surprise.

Once Melba was out of sight, I started looking for my phone book. It took me about thirty minutes to find it in the Bermuda Rectangle. I finally located the thing underneath a clay flowerpot filled with a large philodendron.

The phone book had an ugly damp circle in the middle of its cardboard cover, and the first seven pages or so were soaked through. I evidently had been using the phone book as a kind of coaster whenever I watered the plant. Apparently, I'd remembered to water that philodendron a lot more times than I thought.

All this might sound a tad bit careless, unless you understand that around these parts you don't really have much use for a telephone book, anyway. For one thing, if you don't know somebody's telephone number, you know you'll see them around town sooner or later. For another thing, the book itself is pretty thin. Compared to the phone book in Louisville, for example, the book for Pigeon Fork looks like a pamphlet.

I wiped off its cover, and looked up Delbert Sims. But—just as I suspected—the phone book wasn't much help. His address was listed as Route 1, Box 107. Right. Like I would know where one route ended and another began. And, even if I did, I wasn't about to run around, counting mailboxes.

I'd just picked up the phone to call Vergil Minrath—the sheriff was sure to know where to find Delbert, being as how he must've run Delbert in quite a few times for public intoxication—but I didn't even get the chance to dial. The door to my office was suddenly slammed wide open, the glass in the door rattling as if it were being shaken by a hurricane.

The woman who was standing there on the landing was not going to be winning any beauty contests anytime soon. Right after she started talking, I realized that getting Miss Congeniality was probably out for her, too.

"I been calling you and calling you. Where the heck have you been?" Her unnaturally black hair was pulled back from her face into a hairdo I think they used to call a French twist back in the sixties. It's another one of the hairdos you see in Pigeon Fork that you don't see anywhere else.

The woman with her hair French twisted just stood there for a minute and glared at me. She was wearing deep red lipstick that exactly matched her long red nails. The ruffled red polka-dot dress that she had stuffed her plump self into looked as if she'd found it at a rummage sale. A sale that had been held twenty, maybe thirty years ago.

I smiled at her anyway. A client is a client. I think Gertrude Stein said that. Or something close. "I'm sure sorry I missed your calls," I said. "Is there something I can do for you?"

She was still standing out there on the landing, glaring at me. Fifty if she was a day, she was trying her darnedest to look twenty-five. If the world were lit by candlelight, she might've made it. "You sure don't look like no detective I've ever seen," she said.

"How many have you seen?" I said. I said it a lot more kindly than I really wanted to.

She shrugged. "Are you the one looking into the pet killings?"

I nodded. Evidently she'd heard about it from the same grapevine as Melba. If this kept up, the newspaper was going to be out of business in no time. "Yes, I'm investigating the Turley murder," I said.

The woman on the landing gave me a quick nod. "Turley. Yep, that's the one, all right," she said. She bustled noisily into my office, settling herself into the chair opposite my desk. "Interesting place you got here," she said. When she walked in, she had large tortoiseshell eyeglasses with red rhinestones at the corners dangling by a black rope around her neck. Now she put them on to peer critically around my office. "Yep, real interesting."

Somehow, the way she said the word made me realize instantly that *interesting* was not a compliment. "Is there something I can do for you?" I repeated.

"Nope, there's something I can do for *you*." She gave me a wide smile that revealed a smear of red lipstick across her front teeth. "I'm Emmaline Johnston, and I'm here to tell you that I am right tickled that somebody is finally doing something to catch this monster!"

The minute I heard the name, I groaned inwardly. This was the woman who'd been writing all those letters to the editor of the *Pigeon Fork Gazette*. The one who wanted to have the joint funeral for Grammy and her pets. Oh, brother. I wondered just how long it would take me to get her out of my office. A couple of days, maybe? I gave her a weak smile. "It's very nice of you to drop by, Miss Johnston, but right now—"

She interrupted me. "It's *Miz* Johnston," she said. "Now, listen up, I got some information on that there murder that I think you'll be needing. And you won't have to pay me for it, neither."

What a citizen. I could barely understand a word she was saying because of all the smacking noises she was making. I figured Emmaline must have at least five sticks of chewing gum in her mouth, judging from the way her jaws were working.

"And what information would that be?" I asked.

Emmaline was fishing around in her purse, and pulled out several crumpled notes. "Just take yourself a gander at these," she said.

I took a gander. On my desk were five sheets of ordinary notebook paper, the kind any schoolkid can get a hold of. On every one of these pieces of paper was what looked to be the same very bad handwriting. If you could call it handwriting. The penciled messages were written in all capitals—the way you write when you're still in kindergarten. For some reason, I thought of Joe Eddy.

The first note was blunt.

KEEP YOUR BIG NOSE OUTTA THIS!
IT WERENT YOU'RE CAT!

This one was obviously written by someone of Joe Eddy's all-around brilliance. I particularly liked the misspelling of "your." The writer's English teacher would be proud.

Emmaline jabbed a ruby-tipped finger at the first note. "I got that one right after my first letter to the editor." She ran her hand self-consciously along the

54

side of her head. Not a stray hair was out of place, but she kept rubbing the side of her head anyway. The way you might a cat.

I looked over at the next note. This one's tone had taken a turn for the worse.

> LISTEN, BITCH! IF YOU NO WHATS GOOD FOR YOU, YOU BETTER CUT IT OUT. I MEAN IT.

Emmaline's eyes had followed mine. "That one came next. I'd only written a couple more letters by then. I was trying to get the mayor to call a town meeting. I mean, whoever did this shouldn't be running around loose. I mean, nobody's safe!" She was petting the side of her head again. "I can't even let my kittycats out at night anymore. It isn't safe! Not with this—this sicko on the loose."

I tried to look sympathetic.

Her eyes were very wide. "Do you know what it's like having to keep litter boxes clean for twelve cats? Do you?"

I shook my head no. I didn't have any idea. Nor did I want to find out. In fact, faced with such a prospect, I might've actually considered whittling down the herd. "I imagine it's been quite a strain," I said.

I looked over at the rest of the notes. There were three more, each one nastier than the next. The last note Emmaline handed me was short, but definitely not sweet.

> STOP OR YOURS GONNA DIE.

I read it twice. Was the writer threatening Emmaline or was he threatening something that belonged to her? Her pets, for instance?

That's the thing English teachers don't tell you. That you need to learn punctuation and spelling if for no other reason than when you're penning your next threatening note, your intended victim will be able to figure out precisely what you intend to do to him.

Apparently, however, Emmaline had already realized all the possibilities of this last message. She looked at that note, smacked her gum for emphasis, and said, "I tell you, Mr. Blevins, if anything happened to my Fluffy or to my Lambykins or to my Midnight or to my Josephine or to—"

I interrupted. It looked like her list of current cat residents might rival Pigeon Fork's phone book. "When did this last note arrive?"

"Day before yesterday. Right after the last edition of the *Gazette* came out. I took it over to the sheriff, too, but you know what he said?"

I could imagine.

"He said he couldn't do nothing until a crime was committed." In between the gum smacking you could hear the outrage in Emmaline's voice. "That fool will wait until one of my precious little sweethearts is—is—*dogmeat!*"

Evidently, that was the worst word she could think of.

My next question I put as gently as I could. "If you've been getting this kind of harassment ever since your first letter, why didn't you stop writing?"

It seemed a practical solution.

Emmaline gave me a look of disbelief. "And let some *maniac* boss me around?" She drew herself up, petting her hair again. "Why, he doesn't know who he's dealing with if he thinks that a few notes is going to shut *me* up! That's just not going to work!"

I was very afraid that the letter-writer might have reached the same conclusion.

"Besides," Emmaline went on, "I've been writing letters ever since the murder—almost seven months now—and I've only gotten five measly threatening notes. That just ain't enough to get me to stop!"

This was yet another conclusion the letter-writer might've reached by now. I was beginning to feel a little worried for Emmaline. She might be in more trouble than she knew. "How did you get these notes? Were they mailed or—?"

Emmaline nodded, and reached down to pull a wad of envelopes out of her purse. "They were mailed," she said. "I found every one of them in my mailbox." She put the crumpled envelopes on my desk with a flourish. "Every one of them's got a Pigeon Fork postmark." A loud gum smack punctuated the last word.

I just looked at her. Emmaline was actually acting as if this were a major breakthrough in the case. Somehow, finding out that whoever was sending her these notes was actually somebody who lived right here in town wasn't exactly a surprise. How else did Emmaline think somebody would even have been able to read her letters in the *Pigeon Fork Gazette*, if they didn't live here? The *Gazette* wasn't exactly the sort of paper you'd have mailed to you out of state.

I nodded and tried to look impressed, anyway. What, unfortunately, impressed me more than anything else was how crumpled up all the letters and envelopes were. Emmaline must've been carrying them around in the bottom of her purse for most of the last six months.

"Have you shown these letters to anybody else?" I asked.

Emmaline nodded her head eagerly. "I showed them to the sheriff, of course. But he acted like it was nothing. He said he thought it could be just a prank." She petted her hair again. "And so, after that, I showed them to everybody—the girls in the Ladies' Auxiliary, and the folks at the library and at the hardware store, and—"

I held up my hand. I got the picture. No doubt the fingerprints of everyone in Pigeon Fork were on these letters and envelopes by now.

I must've looked disapproving because Emmaline started acting huffy. "Well, I wanted everybody to know what that maniac's been up to! And how nobody's doing anything about it. It's an outrage! I mean, this turkey's a murderer and he's threatening *me!*"

I didn't quite follow her line of reasoning. Apparently, to Emmaline's way of thinking, murderers had gall. Not only killing people and animals, but *threatening* people, too. The nerve.

I gave her back her notes and envelopes. "Listen, Ms. Johnston," I said, "if you get another one of these letters, call me right away. Okay? Just leave it in your mailbox and call me."

Emmaline smacked her gum a couple of times, and stared at me. "You know, that's what Sheriff Minrath told me. But I thought he was just trying to get rid of me. He certainly didn't act like it was anything important." She sounded injured.

"Well, I think it's important," I said. "And I'd like to see the next one when it comes. Okay? Don't touch it, though."

"Oh, I can't promise that," Emmaline immediately said, shaking her head emphatically. Not a black hair moved. She must've had enough hairspray on her head to make her hair into black papier-mâché. "No sirree,'" she said. "I can't just leave my mail in my mailbox. My mailbox leaks something awful, you know, and if it rains, my mail could get soaked." She was still shaking her head. "Oh no, I surely couldn't just leave my mail in—"

I interrupted. "How about putting the envelope in a plastic bag? Okay?"

Emmaline looked at me as if measuring me for a straitjacket. "You mean, in a freezer bag? Like you put up corn in?"

I nodded. "That would be fine."

She mulled that one over for a second, her eyes behind the tortoiseshell rims looking oddly out of focus. Then she brightened suddenly as the reason for all this hit her. "Why, you want to look for finger-prints!" At the very same instant she realized, of course, what she'd done to all the other letters. Her face fell. "Oh," she said, looking back at the crumpled papers in her hand.

I smiled at her insincerely. "Now, don't you worry," I said. "It can't be helped now. Besides, we don't even know for sure if the same person who wrote these letters actually committed the murder." I didn't say it, but as far as I knew, it could very easily have been someone who was just sick of seeing Emmaline Johnston's name in print. Having met Emmaline, I could certainly understand that kind of attitude.

My comment had been meant to make Emmaline feel better about wantonly destroying evidence, but she acted as if I'd insulted her. "What?" she said, smacking her gum again. "Well, of course, the notes are from the murderer! I never heard of such a thing. Who else would be sending me hate mail?"

The answer to that one, of course, was probably half the population of Pigeon Fork. But I kept my mouth shut.

"You're just as bad as Sheriff Minrath!" Emmaline said. "Acting just like all this is nothing. The sheriff actually had the colossal nerve to insinuate that I might've written these notes myself! Just to get attention. Well, I told him a thing or two—"

I hadn't thought of that. It was possible that Emmaline was fabricating the entire thing. She certainly seemed capable of it. However, for right now, I had to say something. Emmaline was working herself up something awful—petting her hair, smacking her gum, stuffing the letters back in her purse. "Hey now, don't get me wrong," I said soothingly. "I do believe you're being threatened by a sicko. I really do. I think you're in terrible danger."

She calmed down. She smacked her gum only once before she said, "Well, now, that's more like it."

"And," I added, "I'm going to try my best to find—"

She didn't let me finish. "Try, shmy. Phooey on that. I don't want you to *try*. I want you to catch this creep." All the time she was saying this, she was pointing her finger at me. Like my first-grade teacher used to do, when I got behind on my reading.

I nodded. Back in the first grade, when that teacher kept pointing her finger at me, I couldn't help myself. I bit it. Just a nip. Her finger hadn't bled or anything. Biting her had just been one of those irresistible impulses—an impulse that a spanking from both the school principal *and* my father had failed to make me regret. Now, watching Emmaline's finger wag in front of my face made me remember just how irresistible that impulse had been.

I shut my eyes, hoping it looked like a blink.

"You got something in your eye?" Emmaline said, her own eyes narrowing. She did, however, put her finger away.

"A bit of dust, probably," I lied.

Emmaline was on her feet by then, preparing to bustle her way out the door. "Well, I'll be on my way now," she said, taking off her glasses. "You be sure and call me if you find out anything." I could hear her gum smacking all the way down the stairs.

As if on cue, my phone rang just as Emmaline Johnston's gum smacking faded away. The second I picked up the phone, I recognized the voice. It was wispy, hesitant, fearful—the way a kicked puppy might sound.

"Mr. Blevins?" Eunice Krebbs sounded as if she were looking over her shoulder the entire time she was talking. "Look, I—I didn't want you to get the wrong impression."

"About what?" I asked. If she started trying to convince me that Joe Eddy was really a sensitive soul, it was going to be hard to swallow. Especially after what Melba had just told me.

"A-about Grammy," Eunice said. "Joe Eddy made her sound like she was—like she was not right."

"Not right?" What on earth was she talking about?

There was a short pause, and then the wispy voice went on. "Like Grammy wasn't right in the head."

Now that she mentioned it, that was precisely the impression I had gotten, no doubt about it.

"Well, I—I don't want you going around telling people that," Eunice hurried on. "It just ain't so, and—and Grammy was real proud. It would hurt her real bad if she knew her name was being muddied up now that she's gone." Eunice sounded as if she were near tears.

I felt real sorry for her. Her life sure didn't sound any too great, and yet, she seemed more worried about her late grandmother's reputation than she was about herself. "Eunice, I won't be saying anything about that to anybody," I said. "I mean it."

"Do you promise—" Eunice started to say, but there was a sound like a door slam in back of her. Her voice abruptly changed. "I've got to go," she whispered.

"Eunice—" I said. I was going to tell her not to worry, but I didn't get the chance. The dial tone sounded in my ear.

CHAPTER

FIVE

Instead of phoning the sheriff, I decided to just mosey on down there. Make it look like I wasn't doing anything more than just dropping in for a little chat with an old friend. Vergil and I are fairly friendly on account of his being such a good friend of my dad's at one time—but I don't ever want to push it too far.

Even when he and I worked on the Feedsack Caper together, Vergil seemed a little bit put off at first. Like maybe he wasn't any too keen on some young whippersnapper coming back into town from Louisville, showing him how to do his job.

I could understand how Vergil might not cotton to me horning in on his territory. So I wanted to keep things looking casual. That's why I decided not to phone. Around these parts, folks figure that if it's important enough to actually warrant a phone call, then it must be real urgent.

I sure didn't want Vergil thinking that. He might

start worrying that I was trying to do his work for him. Or worse, that I was after his job.

That would be the day. The idea of spending my Fridays and Saturdays keeping all the Delbert Simses in Pigeon Fork from killing each other—and me—didn't sound like any too great a way to make a living. Vergil was welcome to it.

It took me about ten minutes to mosey on down to the sheriff's office. I could've gotten there faster, but moseying takes time. It was one of them sparkling clear autumn days that we get a lot of here in Pigeon Fork. It was still warm enough to walk around town without a jacket, and I ambled along, taking deep breaths, noticing how much the trees were changing color. It's days like this that make me real glad I'm back here.

Pigeon Fork hasn't changed a whole lot since I was a kid. Oh, there are more stores downtown than there used to be, and the cost of street parking has gone up—from five cents an hour to a dime—but downtown still looks pretty much as I remember it. Large maple trees, wooden park benches, and old-fashioned parking meters still line both sides of Main Street. The Crayton Courthouse Building still looks the same—red brick with a clock tower on top. I don't ever remember that clock working. As far as I know, in Pigeon Fork it's been four-thirty all my life.

Right next to the courthouse is Crayton Federal Bank, with its long narrow windows always closed against the sun, and right next to the bank is the Pigeon Fork Funeral Home, by far the biggest building in town, and one of very few that has an electric sign. I reckon there's a lesson there, but I don't want to even think about what it might be.

The courthouse, the bank and the rest are all on the

other side of the street from Elmo's Drugstore and me. On my side of the street, I went past the Pigeon Fork Dry Goods Store, past Arndell's New and Hardly Used Furniture, past Lassiter's Restaurant, and finally past Pop's Barbershop at the end of the block. Pop's still has one of them old-fashioned red-and-white-striped barber poles out front. You can tell Pop Matheny is real proud of that pole because he's always out front cleaning it with Windex. Today was no exception. Pop lifted his hand in a wave as I went by. I waved back, and went on.

That's something else I've had to get used to, since I've been back. I'd forgotten how people always wave at you out in the country. Here in Pigeon Fork folks wave at you at the drop of a hat.

I figure this waving thing is a holdover from a time not too far back when these parts were real sparsely populated. Back then you could probably go for days without seeing another human being. Just cows and pigs and more cows and pigs. So that when you finally ran across another person, you'd throw up your hand in grateful recognition.

On the way to the sheriff's, I picked up four more waves and a couple of nods. Most of them were from people I recognized—Zeke Arndell, the Lassiter brothers, and Leroy Putnam, who owns the dry goods store—but a couple of the others, though, I'd swear were total strangers.

I don't know why, but it's kind of nice having strangers wave at you. I may have only been back in town four months, but sometimes it feels like the eight years I spent in Louisville never happened.

I was smiling when I opened the door to the sheriff's office. I saw Vergil right away. He was sitting at his big oak rolltop desk, poring over the Louisville *Courier-Journal*.

You can't get the *Courier* home delivered this far from Louisville, but you can pick it up at the grocery store every morning. A lot of people do. Mainly, because if you depended on the *Pigeon Fork Gazette* for world news, you might as well forget it. The United States could've been at war three or four days before it made the *Gazette*. Which, come to think of it, is a real comforting thought.

Scissors in hand, Vergil glanced up the minute I walked in. "Haskell," he said. He turned back to the paper, clipping out a coupon for Dr Pepper—25 cents off a 2-liter bottle.

I nodded. "Vergil," I said. Just saying somebody's name in Pigeon Fork is the same as saying hello. I tried doing the same thing when I lived in Louisville, but nobody seemed to get it. Every single time, the person I was talking to always looked back at me expectantly and said, "What?"

I eased myself into the chair opposite Vergil's desk, and watched him clip. Vergil didn't look back up at me until he'd carefully cut out a coupon for vegetable soup, and one for buttermilk biscuits. I watched him fondly.

Vergil and my dad were best friends in high school. In fact, I can't remember a time when I didn't know Vergil. If my dad were still alive, he and Vergil would both be fifty-eight this year. Only Vergil's always looked older. Vergil's got salt and pepper hair—what there is left of it—and a fairly good-sized gut on him. It's kind of ironic, I reckon, that my dad—who always looked the youngest—was the one who had a heart attack when he was just forty-nine. It happened, though, the year after my mom died of cancer.

I've always figured Dad just couldn't live without her.

Vergil added his newly clipped coupons to the growing stack, and looked over at me. No matter what Vergil is doing, he always looks as if he just got back from a funeral. Lines like spider webs crisscross his tanned face, and even when he smiles, the corners of his mouth still manage to turn down. I was still smiling when Vergil looked my way. "How are you doing?" I asked.

Vergil smiled sadly back, laying down his scissors. "Best as I can on my salary."

This is what Vergil always says. No "Fine, thank you," for him. He leaned back in his chair, and sighed. "Eggs are only sixty cents at the Crayton County Supermarket," he said. His tone implied that this was tragic news. "With a coupon, of course," he added.

"Sixty cents?" I said. "No kidding. At the Crayton County Supermarket? Well, I'll sure remember that." Actually, there is nothing super about the Crayton County Supermarket. It's just a big house with a couple of Coke machines and a gasoline pump out front. Inside it's always dark and crowded and smells strongly of ammonia. I prefer to do my shopping at the only other grocery store in town, Higgin's Stop 'n' Shop.

Vergil and I looked at each other. I wondered how to bring up the subject of the Turley case.

"You know what?" Vergil drawled. "Now that I think of it, I do believe Delbert Sims lives in back of the Crayton County Supermarket. He lives in that little stone house right out back."

"You don't say," I said. Vergil is not dumb. In a way, this was a little disheartening. Because if Vergil is this smart, and he hadn't managed to find out who killed Grammy and her pets in seven months, how on earth did I expect to figure it out?

"I reckon you heard, huh?" I said.

Vergil shrugged. His eyes seemed to be looking at the woes of the entire world. "I reckon," he said.

I took a deep breath. Being casual looked out of the question now. "Don't suppose you could tell me something about the Turley case, could you?"

The lines on Vergil's face deepened. He sighed and opened a file drawer on his left. He slapped a thick manila folder down in front of me. "It's all right there—'bout everything I know. But, I warn you, it ain't much." From his manner, he could've been delivering a eulogy.

I tried not to look surprised that Vergil would just hand the folder right over. With no argument or nothing. This was certainly a damn sight easier than I'd expected it to be. I must've not done too good a job at not looking surprised, though, because Vergil said, "Reckon I wouldn't hate having some help on this one. Being as how I've pretty much hit a dead end."

I opened the file, intending to read it from cover to cover, but Vergil wasn't going to let me get on with it as easy as all that, after all. He put a big tanned hand over where I was reading. "This is not to say that we law enforcement officers here in Pigeon Fork need any help on a regular basis from big-city folk." He lifted one gray eyebrow as if to say, Understand?

I nodded. "I reckon you all do fine," I said.

Vergil nodded, leaning back in his chair. He sighed once again. "I reckon we do," he said.

That settled, he let me read.

According to the autopsy report stapled to the left side of the folder, Grammy was killed by a blow from a blunt object. She had been hit twice. The second blow killed her. The murder weapon had never been located.

I flipped real quick through the other papers in the folder. "No autopsy on the animals?"

Vergil's look was reproachful. "I don't know how they generally do things in Louisville, but here in Pigeon Fork we generally confine our autopsies to human beings." He shrugged, a gesture of infinite grief. "Call us old-fashioned."

I smiled at him. "Just wondering," I said. I started to go back to reading.

"And, even if we'd wanted to do an autopsy, we wouldn't have been able to," Vergil went on. He could've been describing the death of a loved one. "Joe Eddy had already buried the animals that same day."

I looked up. There was such a thing as exhuming. But I didn't mention it. What I said was, "That was kind of quick, wasn't it?" Joe Eddy didn't look to me to be the type to do any kind of work with any kind of speed.

Vergil shrugged again. "I don't know. Depends on how long you could stand having a dead cat and a dead parakeet laying around." He gave me another one of his sad looks. "My personal opinion," he said, "is that it was none too soon."

I could see his point.

"You don't happen to know what Joe Eddy does for a living, do you?"

Vergil scratched his bald spot. "Best I could tell, he's a handyman. You know, a jack-of-all-trades." Vergil picked up his scissors and started looking through the *Courier* again. "Must be pretty good at it. Joe Eddy seems to do all right. Better than most."

I could understand why. If I were a housewife living around Pigeon Fork and I called up a handyman, and it turned out to be Joe Eddy who showed up at my door with his toolbox, I'd pay him double *not* to come in. Joe Eddy was probably doing very well indeed.

I turned back to the folder in my hands. In a pocket folder on the right side were several black-and-white glossies of the murder scene. Poor Grammy lay crumpled facedown on the floor exactly where Grampap had shown me. I guess, when something like this happens, every terrible detail is burned right into your mind, never ever to be forgotten. No wonder Grampap had been able to point out the exact spot.

Grammy was wearing a flowered housedress and terry cloth house shoes. Each shoe had a little bow on the toe. The cheerfulness of those little bows made a startling contrast to the dark black pool that had formed at the back of her head. It looked like oil against the gleaming surface of Grampap's immaculate floor.

Beside Grammy's body was the cat, a large tabby with markings like a miniature tiger, its head bloodied. It looked like a large furry fly that had been swatted.

Next to the cat, about three feet away, it looked like, was the parakeet. It had been more than swatted. It had been flattened. Positively flattened. Somehow, looking at that little parakeet pancake was even more unnerving than looking at poor Grammy.

I swallowed and took a deep breath. I've got a dog myself, and while sometimes I've actually considered doing something like this to him—particularly the time he chewed up my brand-new Italian leather boots—

still, seeing it actually done to a pet is a whole other thing.

I glanced away for a second, only to see Vergil looking straight at me. "Kinda awful, ain't it?" he said. For the first time since I'd walked in, his funereal tone was entirely appropriate.

I nodded.

"That right there is another reason we didn't do autopsies on the animals," Vergil said, giving me a level look. "Don't you think—from looking at those pictures—that we could hazard a pretty good guess as to what killed them?" There might have been a trace of sarcasm in Vergil's tone, but I chose to ignore it.

I looked back over at the rest of the photos. There were a couple of black-and-white pictures showing the bodies covered in what looked to be sheets. The bird, it looked like, had been covered with a handkerchief. A couple of feathers poked out at the edge.

For some reason—I don't know why exactly—but when I got to that picture, I wanted to laugh. I know. I'm awful. I moved on to the next picture real quick. This one struck me just as funny. It was one of the outlines on the floor, after the bodies had been taken away. An outline of poor Grammy. One of the cat. And, finally, one of the bird.

My eyes started to water, I was trying so hard not to bust out laughing. I could feel Vergil's somber eyes on my face, but I didn't dare look over at him. Instead, I blinked real fast and hurried on to the other photos.

Thank God, the next pictures were black-and-white glossies of the table, the one I'd already seen so carefully preserved at Grampap's. There was Grammy's diagram of the flower garden, the list of flowers and prices, the seed catalogue. Nothing appreciably different from what I'd already seen. There was a pencil on the floor beside Grammy's outstretched hand, but that seemed to be it. Everything else looked the same.

That was all of the photos. I put them away, with more than a little relief. If I had broken out laughing in front of Vergil, I don't know how I could've explained it. Yes, now that you mention it, Vergil, I do happen to be an insensitive clod. Somehow, I don't think Vergil would be at all willing to work with somebody who thought his murder case was a real knee-slapper.

Next, I read the statements given by Joe Eddy, and Grampap, and Eunice, and they all sounded familiar. Delbert Sims' statement was new. His account dwelt heavily on how much time he spent in the living room with the others. The only time he left was to get more beer, and that was just a matter of minutes. Minutes. He kept saying that, over and over and over.

No mention was made of his being engaged at one time to the victim. In fact, Delbert made it sound as if he barely knew Grammy—that his friendship was mainly with Grampap Turley and Joe Eddy.

He did admit that he hated her pets. "Pesky varmints," he called them. "Always underfoot, or flying around your head. Can't say I could see why she kept them filthy pets around. I'd have shot both of them a long time ago."

That was blunt. I wondered if Delbert had been drunk when he admitted such a thing to the sheriff. It didn't seem likely that he would have said that if he'd been sufficiently sober to realize its implications.

Vergil was adding yet another coupon to his pile when I looked up next. "Have you ever heard anything about two people named Ray Don Peters or Myrldean Bleemel?" I asked.

Vergil just looked at me, puzzled. "Well, now, let me see, Ray Don Peters died about a year ago. It made the front page of the *Gazette*. I reckon you don't remember it because you were still living in Louisville back then." Did I imagine it, or was Vergil's tone faintly accusing? "As I recall, Ray Don fell down his basement stairs," Vergil went on. "Coroner ruled it an accident." He paused and reached into one of his file drawers for another manila folder.

Vergil looked at the folder a minute or so, and turned back to me. "As for Myrldean Bleemel," Vergil said, "she died about two years ago. Also, ruled an accident. Says here she fell down her front steps, hit her head on the pavement."

Vergil waited a full thirty seconds before he asked, "Why did you want to know?"

I shrugged. "Their names were mentioned, is all. I wondered if their deaths could be related in some way. I mean, they were all friends of Grammy's."

Vergil gave me a skeptical stare. "You mean to tell me you think there might be some kind of serial killer here in Pigeon Fork? Murdering old people?" He had the decency to swallow his laugh. "How do you account for the bird and parakeet? Was the cat old in cat-years? Or maybe the bird was getting on up there in bird-years?"

Vergil can really make you feel small. He's been doing this to me ever since I really was small. I just smiled weakly at him, as if I had completely missed the contempt in his voice. "It was just a thought, Vergil. That's all," I said. "I mean, they *were* all acquainted—"

Vergil shook his head. "Everybody in Pigeon Fork

is acquainted. There isn't a single old person here who doesn't know all the other old people here. It's a small town, Haskell.''

I hate it when he starts this. *Instructing* me, just as if I were six years old again. Next, he'll be telling me how to tie my shoelaces.

I gave Vergil another weak smile. "A small town, you say? Small, huh? No kidding," I said.

Vergil stared back at me, his eyes still sad, and turned back to his coupons. I turned back to the folder. Vergil had even included in the Turley file photocopies of every one of Emmaline Johnston's letters to the editor. They were the main reason the file was so fat. I looked up when I got through skimming those. "What do you make of Emmaline Johnston?"

Vergil finished cutting out another one of his coupons before he answered. This one was for Kleenex, buy one box, get one free. "Let me see. A busybody do-gooder who's nuts about cats. That about cover it?"

"Pretty much," I said. "What do you make of the letters she's been getting?"

Vergil sighed yet again. If they ever make sighing an Olympic event, Vergil has a shot at the gold medal. "Maybe Emmaline's letters are from the killer, maybe not." He scratched his bald spot again—this time with the scissors. You'd think that would hurt. Vergil didn't even wince. "Emmaline could be writing them herself," he said, "—or maybe somebody in town could've run out of patience and be trying to shut her up." Vergil paused then and leaned forward. "Made me suspicious, though, when I asked Emmaline to bring me one of them letters without handling it first—and she never did."

I nodded. It did sound a little suspicious. It could be, however, that Emmaline just didn't have much faith in Vergil's crime-stopping abilities.

Vergil started to go back to his coupon clipping, but I had another question. "Was there anybody who knew Grammy and also hated animals?"

Vergil didn't even hesitate. "Delbert Sims. From what I hear, he doesn't like animals much. Fact is, I don't think Delbert likes anything much that doesn't come out of a bottle."

Vergil stopped for a minute and then added, "Not that you can completely blame old Delbert. I hear tell that them pets even got on Grammy's nerves sometime."

"What?"

Vergil nodded. "Sure enough. One of the parcel post deliverymen heard Grammy screaming something awful at her cat one time. It had evidently been doing its business in her flowers."

"When was this?"

Vergil shrugged. "Couple of months before Grammy died." Vergil's eyes traveled back to the paper. "Grammy could cuss like a sailor, believe it or not."

I tried to put a casual "Oh, really?" sort of look on my face, but evidently what showed up was an amazed "You are kidding me!"

Vergil nodded his head, his eyes even sadder. "Grammy wasn't exactly the perfect lady," he said.

This was getting more and more interesting. "You knew Grammy?" I asked. "Personally?"

Vergil shrugged. "I saw her every once in a while. She was a real flirt. Shameless. And her a married woman and all."

I didn't know how to take that. For one thing, ever since Vergil's wife of thirty-one years walked out on their marriage a couple of years ago, Vergil has been

75

a tad bit sour on women. I can't imagine why his wife left him—he must be such a joy to have around—but I would never even hint to Vergil that I might see her viewpoint.

Besides, in a way, I don't. Doris—that's Vergil's ex-wife—had to know he wasn't exactly a barrel of laughs when she married him. So, why did he suddenly get to be intolerable after thirty-one years, for Christ's sake?

No wonder Vergil is a little down on women. He and I are somewhat alike in this respect, I guess. After four years of living with Claudine—I call her Claudzilla—I'm a little down on women myself. Only Vergil is worse than I am. He's pretty mad at all women. Me, I still love women. It's wives I've got a problem with.

Knowing how Vergil feels about women in general made me take what he said with a grain of salt. Actually, the entire box of salt was what I took it with. "You think Grammy was running around on her husband?" I asked.

Vergil gave me an "Are you stupid?" look. "Not a doubt in my mind." He was talking as if he were at a funeral again. "Women don't advertise if they're not on the market." Vergil cocked his head at me as if he'd just quoted the Bible to me.

"You have any idea who she might've been playing around with?"

"I reckon I do," Vergil said.

"And—?" Sometimes, getting Vergil to say anything is worse than pulling teeth. It's more like digging them out with a spoon.

"Delbert Sims," Vergil finally said, his sad gray eyes locked on mine. "That's my guess. They were seen together a lot."

"You mean, like kissing or holding hands or—"

Vergil cut me off. "I mean, like talking in the grocery, acting real cozy, walking out together after church. They weren't stupid enough to carry on in public, but from what I've heard and seen, you could tell something was going on."

It was my turn to look sad now. Did Vergil expect me to believe that the *grocery* and *church* were hot spots for romance these days? Was he kidding?

"Then you think this might've been a lovers' quarrel kind of thing?" I asked.

Vergil nodded solemnly.

"Then I guess Delbert might be your prime suspect?"

Vergil took up his scissors again. "Might be," he said.

Somehow, the vision of Grammy as a philandering wife didn't quite mesh with the image I'd had of her up to now. I mean, was there such a thing as a sixty-six-year-old trollop? And, if there were, do sixty-six year-old trollops wear flowered housedresses and terry cloth house shoes? I always thought philandering wives wore silk negligees and satin mules. That's what mine wore, anyway.

Still, Grammy did look remarkably young for her age. Maybe philandering was what kept her young. If it was, I doubted very much that this particular secret of eternal youth would be mentioned in one of those stay-young books that are always on the market.

I left Vergil still looking mournfully through the *Courier,* and headed back toward my office. I had parked my truck, as always, in the alleyway to the right of the drugstore. For some reason, just as I was about to begin the climb to my office, I looked over at my truck.

And I noticed something white fluttering on my windshield.

I think I knew even before I got to my truck what it was. How many flyers do you get printed on a folded piece of notebook paper? I eased the paper out from under my windshield wiper, touching it only on one corner. Inside, sure enough, was the familiar terrible handwriting. Also familiar was the lousy English and the equally lousy spelling.

The contents of the note certainly lacked originality.

KEEP YOUR BIG NOSE OUTA THIS. IT AINT ANY OF YOUR BIZNESS.

Right after I finished reading that excellent example of a lack of education in the basics, I noticed something else. My truck seemed to be leaning to one side.

I went around the other side, already beginning not to be in my best mood. After I got a good look, I was certain of it. My best mood was out of the question. But, just in case the letter-writer was watching me, from some concealed advantage, I didn't say one curse word. Not one.

I also didn't kick my truck, or throw a little fit. All of which it occurred to me to do. As a matter of fact, I think I showed remarkable control.

Considering that both my tires on the left side had been slashed.

CHAPTER

SIX

Pigeon Fork may be a small town, but when most of its population is standing in the alley next to Elmo's Drugstore, it makes quite a crowd. I recognized Zeke Arndell, Pop Matheny, the Lassiters, the Putnams—in fact, it looked like nearly every downtown business was represented. Vergil, of course, was also there, along with one of his deputies.

I had at least a passing acquaintance with most of the folks standing there in the alley, but some of the men in bib overalls and polyester suits I'm pretty sure I'd never seen before. Not to mention several of the women in housedresses and knit pants.

All of these folks were milling around, talking animatedly among themselves and pointing overy once in a while to what was left of my tires. There was a kind of carnival atmosphere in the air. Quite a few kids had shown up, being as how school had just let out a few minutes before. I recognized Melba's oldest three. All these youngsters, including Melba's, were darting in and out of the crowd, giggling and snickering.

79

My shredded tires had become a Pigeon Fork community event.

My brother Elmo was also standing in the alley. He was, as usual, looking worried. "I told you, Haskell, you're a-going to get yourself hurt."

Elmo is four years older than me, but we look a lot alike. He's about my height and weight, but he doesn't have my assortment of freckles. I think that's how come nobody compares him to Howdy Doody.

He does have my red hair, though. It makes an orangey-red border around his ears and the back of his head. From a distance he looks as if his furry orange earmuffs have slipped.

The top of Elmo's head, unfortunately, doesn't have any earmuffs, orange or not. In fact, Elmo has exactly nineteen hairs left up there. I counted them one Sunday afternoon when Elmo happened to fall asleep on my couch while watching a football game on my TV.

It is my considered opinion that Elmo's hair fell out because he worries so much—all that extra energy radiating from his brain burned up his roots.

Elmo's nineteen hairs are worn in the latest style for bald men—letting them grow very long and then combing them across. Elmo apparently believes that this is the perfect camouflage. I don't have the heart to tell him any different.

I also don't stare at Elmo's head anymore, the way I used to. Nowadays, I can talk to Elmo for hours without once looking at his nineteen hairs. Now that's self-control.

I was not looking at the top of his head as Elmo went worriedly on. "If'n you don't find yourself another line of work, mark my words, Haskell, you're a-going to regret it."

PET PEEVES

Elmo has been after me, ever since I moved back to Pigeon Fork, to join the thrill-packed world of drugstore management. I don't want to hurt his feelings, since he seems real happy in his work. But, frankly, I consider plumbing more exciting. "I appreciate your concern," I told Elmo.

Elmo frowned at me, looked pointedly at my butchered tires, and went on back inside his drugstore. He was doing a pretty brisk business in there, selling ice-cream cones, soft drinks and potato chips to everybody who'd shown up to discuss my tire tragedy.

As soon as Elmo left, Melba suddenly appeared. I'm sure it wasn't any accident that she didn't show up while Elmo was still talking to me. It's a game the two of them play. The object for Melba is to stay out of Elmo's sight just in case he's got some work for her to do. The object for Elmo is to catch her avoiding him. I used to play this game with my mom when I was a kid. Melba is real good at it.

"So what do you think?" Melba said, jerking her head over at my tires. At the same time as Melba was tilting her beehive toward my truck, she was taking a big lick off a vanilla ice-cream cone. Her eye–hand coordination must be amazing.

"Well, I think my tires are flat," I said, looking at her real steady. I wasn't about to give her an opening.

Melba didn't bat an eyelash. She took another big lick off her cone and said, "You think it was the same perp who iced the old lady?"

Oh Lord. I knew it. Melba was doing her Della Street impression again. I took a deep breath. "I don't have any idea, Melba," I said through my teeth. "You didn't happen to see anybody out here in the alley earlier today, did you?" I'd asked Elmo the same thing, but he'd shook his head.

81

Melba didn't shake her head. Instead, she took another big lick off her cone. It was a good move on her part. That cone was starting to drip. After licking it real good, Melba held the cone out a ways so that it wouldn't drip on her dress. "Nope," she finally said. "I reckon it must've happened when I was on my break."

That I believed. As best as I could tell, Melba's workday was about 90 percent break.

"So, Chief, do you suppose Joe Eddy followed you back into town and did this to scare you off?" Melba stared around us at the crowd, her small blue eyes getting even smaller. "Or do you think the perp was somebody else? Maybe somebody right *here*, right under our very noses, gloating over what he's done!"

Melba's voice was pretty loud. I had no intention of standing there, in the middle of that crowd, discussing possible culprits. "Melba," I said, "this is hardly the place—"

She interrupted me, stepping up right next to me so that a drip from her cone barely missed my shoes. "I could nose around, if you want." Her round nose actually twitched when she said that. "I mean, I could do a little talking around town, see if I could get the straight skinny on Joe Eddy and Eunice and Grampap Turley—"

I just stared at her. You'd think Melba would have all she could handle, holding down a job and raising five kids. Melba, though, told me once that she was a what you call "laissez-faire" mother. I looked that up in one of them French-American dictionaries. It means "let them alone." That's sure what Melba does, all right. She lets her kids alone while they're doing God knows what to everybody else. Right that minute Melba's thirteen-year-old and eleven-year-old were chasing her nine-year-old through the crowd, laughing and carrying on. Every once in a while one of the three would plow into somebody, or else trip and fall. No matter what happened, their response was always the same. All three laughed even louder.

Melba didn't even glance in her kids' direction. Her eyes were riveted on my face. "I could just ask me a few questions here and there," she said. "And don't you worry. I'll tell everybody I'm working for you. I'm not out to steal your thunder."

My head started thundering then. The idea of Melba running all over town asking questions of everybody and anybody was enough to give me a headache. For one thing, I wasn't sure Melba would even know the questions to ask. For another, didn't something like this take some semblance of subtlety? Melba's questioning would, no doubt, be like performing surgery with a meat cleaver.

"No, Melba," I said, trying to sound firm—maybe even threatening—"I'd rather do the talking to folks myself. Understand?"

Melba just looked at me, letting her cone drip. And drip. I shuffled my feet a little, moving further out of the way. "Really, Haskell." Melba's voice was huffy. "I don't see what harm just asking a few little bitty questions could possibly do. I just want to help out on this case. That's all I want."

I stared back at her. Now wait a minute. Hold the phone. This was serious. Melba was not getting the message. And I couldn't have Melba *helping*. Melba's help would, no doubt, be anything but. Lord. "Melba," I said, "I mean it, I *do not* want you to talk to anybody about this case. *Do you hear?* I mean it, *nobody*. Do you—" I didn't get to finish because Vergil came up then, and when Melba saw the look on the sheriff's face, she sort of melted into the crowd, licking on her cone again.

Vergil looked furious. He stood there, staring at my mangled tires, shifting his weight from one scuffed boot to another, doing a pretty good imitation of a volcano about to explode.

I was touched. I was just thinking how nice it was of Vergil, him taking this so personally and all, and obviously feeling so outraged on my behalf when Vergil said, his frown deepening, "Well, Haskell, I do believe I'm insulted."

"Insulted?" I said.

"You bet I am." Vergil's tone was not kind. "I been working on the Turley case for seven months now, and nobody's slashed *my* tires."

I just looked at him. He wasn't kidding. "Well, if it wasn't for the honor of the thing," I said, "I would've just as soon skipped it."

Vergil didn't even crack a smile. Not that I really expected him to. Smiles are not exactly in Vergil's repertoire of facial expressions.

Minutes ago I'd watched Vergil putting the note I found on my windshield in a plastic evidence bag. Now he waved the bag at me, accusingly. "—and I haven't received even one note," he went on. "Not a single note in seven months!" Vergil made a derisive noise in the back of his throat.

With that note waving in my face, I didn't know what to say. I was beginning to consider sending Vergil a threatening note myself. It would certainly make me feel better, and I had no doubt that it would do Vergil a world of good.

Vergil stopped waving the note at me, and settled for just glaring. "I reckon I'll be sending this evidence on up to the state lab," he said. He pronounced the word, "evvy-denz."

Vergil then sighed heavily and added, "It'll take the lab a while to make hide or hair of who could've sent this to you. Might be a couple of days or more before we get it back." As always, Vergil was still looking as if he'd just walked out of a funeral. Only this time his grief was tempered some. Like maybe he'd hated whoever had died.

I nodded at him. "Well, I sure appreciate your looking into this for me, Vergil." Actually, I was feeling a tad irritated. It sure wasn't *my* fault that somebody had chosen my truck to vandalize, or that they'd picked my windshield to leave their bad English on. If I'd been given a choice, I would've volunteered Vergil's truck and windshield for the purpose. Without even thinking twice.

Vergil probably saw all that in my eyes, because he turned abruptly and started heading back toward his office. He'd taken only about two steps, though, when he stopped and turned back to me. "Sorry about your truck, Haskell."

I don't think I've ever heard words spoken with less sincerity.

There is, however, justice in this world. Vergil had no sooner started moving away from me, in the direction of his office, when Melba suddenly appeared and went running after him. She must've been standing, just out of sight, waiting for her chance. "Oh, Vergil," she said. Her voice was lilting. "I reckon you'll be a-wanting to take *my* statement now, won't you?" She fluttered her heavily mascaraed eyes at him.

Vergil's eyes got wide. "Uh, uh, uh—" That Vergil, he's got a real way with the ladies.

I watched Melba move in for the kill, trying hard not to smile.

"You will be needing to question me, won't you?" Melba put a plump hand possessively on Vergil's forearm. "I mean, I *am* a witness."

"Uh, uh, uh—" Vergil repeated. That man is some conversationalist. I could take lessons from him.

Melba's eyes narrowed. "You do want to talk to me, don't you?"

All the while Melba was talking, Vergil had been looking wildly around, no doubt trying to locate his deputy. His deputy, however, had wisely disappeared. Vergil finally sighed, looking as though maybe what he really wanted to do was ask for a blindfold and a last cigarette. "I—I reckon so," he said to Melba. "I guess I will be needing to know what you saw."

Melba smiled so wide you could see the fillings in her back teeth. "Well, come on inside, then, you big handsome thing," Melba said. "I'll fix us some coffee and tell you all about it."

Melba and the sheriff started to move inside. "I think you'll be real interested in what I got to tell you," Melba cooed.

The sheriff shot me a look. It was the look a drowning man might give a life raft.

I looked away. "Well," I said, not to anybody in particular, just in general, "I reckon I better get on up to my office. Got to get these here tires fixed." I turned back then and smiled at Vergil and Melba both.

Vergil's eyes got even bigger.

"Do you take cream and sugar in your coffee?" Melba said, leading her prey inside.

Vergil refused to budge for a second. He looked over at me and soundlessly mouthed the word *help*.

I pretended not to understand, and started toward my office.

Just so you know I'm not totally heartless, on my way upstairs, I did feel a little twinge of guilt. I immediately dismissed it, though. There wasn't anything I could've done, anyway.

When Melba has a man in her sights, she's sort of like that big white shark in those Jaws movies. Once that shark had got a hold of somebody, you knew it had him. It wasn't ever going to let the guy go. Sure as shootin', if you tried to rescue the guy, you only endangered yourself.

Besides, I was feeling kind of relieved that Vergil had, for the time being anyway, taken Melba's mind off of "helping" me. There was no doubt about it. I was going to have to give her a good talking-to. I was going to have to make it crystal clear that we were not now—nor would we ever be—business partners. And that I would always be able to do my own questioning, thank you, all by myself.

How I was going to get that point across, however, short of hitting Melba between the eyes with a two-by-four, was something else again.

It took me the rest of the day to get my tires replaced. I called up the McAfee Brothers Service Station the minute I walked into my office, but they didn't show up for another forty-five minutes. Even though their service station is just three blocks away.

The McAfees are the Pigeon Fork equivalent of Ma Bell. They've got the only full-service garage in town. Their motto, I think, is: When you've got a monopoly, why try harder? The McAfees will get you those full services whenever they damn well feel like it. And not a minute sooner.

The sun was going down by the time the McAfees

were in the mood to give me back my truck. It was too late by then to do any talking to Delbert Sims. He was probably too drunk by sundown to be able to actually form entire words, anyway, so I gave up on it. I just headed on home.

Home these days is five acres of wooded hills about seven miles outside of the Pigeon Fork city limits. I live in a small A-frame right in the middle of one of them hills. To get there, you have to go up a real steep gravel driveway for about a quarter of a mile, which everybody who's ever visited me complains about.

I don't mind it myself. Of course, my truck does have four-wheel drive. And I really like the privacy. That steep driveway of mine pretty much guarantees that whoever is visiting me is somebody I want to see. I don't get any Avon ladies or Jehovah's Witnesses dropping by.

As soon as I started up my driveway, my dog Rip started barking. Rip doesn't get much practice barking at trespassers, so he evidently decided a long time ago that he'd put in his barking time whenever *I* showed up.

It's a real annoying thing to have your own dog barking at you. Like maybe sometime during the day he forgot you live there, too.

All the time I was pulling my truck into the garage, Rip kept on barking. He'd calm down a bit, like maybe he was winding down, and then he'd be at it again louder than ever. Rip is the third dog I've ever owned—the other two never barked at me.

On the other hand, the other two both died before they were a year old. For a while there, I was having some real bad luck with dogs. Seemed like every time

I got myself one, it would come down with something fatal.

I was always real careful, too. I always got my dogs all their shots, always had them checked out by the vet—and still they died. That's why I named Rip what I did. I'd gotten so used to my dogs dying, that right after I got this new puppy, I just put R.I.P. on his doghouse.

Rip, however, is six years old now. I think he's going to live. A big black half-shepherd, half-no-telling-what, he stopped barking as soon as I started walking up the steps to my front door. I could almost see the light dawning in Rip's brown eyes. *Oh yeah. Now I remember. It's the guy who feeds me.* His barking done, Rip started wagging his tail and jumping in the air as if all day long he'd been pining away for me.

"Good dog, Rip, good boy, how are you doing, boy?" I said. Rip wagged harder, getting as close as he dared to the edge of the steps.

My entire house is surrounded by a large deck, so you have to climb quite a few steps to get to my front door. Except for Rip, of course. Rip won't go up and down steps. I've actually tried coaxing him downstairs with pieces of steak, but that fool dog still refuses to budge.

It's my opinion that Rip was traumatized as a puppy, before I ever got him. How it happened, I'll never know. Maybe his mom dragged him up and down stairs, bumping him on every step. Whatever it was that got done to him, Rip is what you call psychologically scarred, according to the vet.

This is something, of course, that I knew about Rip before I ever moved him and me out here, but I guess I didn't exactly think it through. All I thought about was what a wonderful view I had of all those trees out on that wraparound deck.

Something else should've occurred to me.

Rip calmed down when I got to the top step. He sat there and waited patiently for me to pick him up. And, yes, carry him down all those steps to the yard. This dog weighs about fifty pounds now. Picking him up is like hoisting a feedsack.

But how can you get mad at the mentally ill? At least Rip is real good about not making a mess on my deck. I figure he's either got one huge bladder, or he's got remarkable self-control.

Once Rip did his business and I'd carried him back upstairs, I started up dinner. I hadn't even put the steak on the grill, though, when my phone rang.

"Haskell?" It was a familiar voice. The kind you pour on pancakes. "It's Cordelia Turley," the voice said. "I saw you in your office earlier today?"

Did she think I'd forget *her* this quick? How many cases did she think I was working on? "Yes?" I said.

"Did you have time today to talk with anybody?" Cordelia sounded anxious.

Somehow, yes, I had managed to squeeze a few chats into my busy schedule. Lord knows how I did it. "Why, yes, I did," I said.

I told her real quick who all I'd talked to, and went through some of the things I'd found out. I even told her about my talk with Emmaline Johnston, about the threatening notes Emmaline had received, and how anxious Emmaline was to have this case solved now that she was having to keep all her cats indoors. Cordelia actually snickered a little at that.

I left out, however, what I'd found out about the particulars of the actual murder itself—it didn't seem necessary to go into all that with Cordelia. No use upsetting her.

I did tell her about my tires, though. Not to make her feel bad or anything, just to let her know that we were making somebody nervous almost immediately.

"Oh, my goodness, that's terrible!" Cordelia sounded shocked. "Oh, Haskell, I am *so* sorry."

I shrugged before I realized that there was no one there who could see me shrug except Rip. He was looking at me as if I were out of my mind. He looks at me that way a lot. The dog who won't go up and down steps. "It's okay," I told Cordelia. "My tires are all fixed now. It was no big thing."

"You'll have to add your tires to your list of expenses," Cordelia said.

I didn't argue. Call me mercenary.

Cordelia then paused and said, "So, what do you think?"

Good grief. Did she expect me to tell her who killed her grandmother tonight? I was good, but I wasn't *that* good. "Well," I said, "I think it's going to be real hard to find out who killed your grandmother after seven months have passed." I had to be honest with her. I wasn't a miracle worker.

"Oh," she said. Her voice was real flat. "Then you think it's hopeless?"

"Well, now, I didn't say that."

"Oh," she said again. This time she sounded a lot happier. "Then you *are* going to try—"

"I am," I said. "I'm going to talk to Delbert Sims tomorrow. And—" Here I hesitated, my heart starting to beat a little faster. "—and, I think we should discuss what I find out over dinner tomorrow night."

I said this last part real fast before I lost courage. It

seemed as if I totally stopped breathing until she answered.

"Why, sure," Cordelia said, without hesitating even a second. She went on to tell me that she was staying at Robey's Boarding House, that she'd be ready at seven, and that—as they say—was that.

I hung up the phone, feeling as if I might start jumping in the air just like old Rip. In sheer joy. Until a thought occurred to me.

Do you suppose Cordelia didn't realize that I was asking her out on a date? Maybe she was under the impression that this was some kind of business dinner. Maybe she thought this was a client–detective conference of some kind, with food thrown in for good measure.

My ex-wife Claudine always said I didn't know one thing about women. There was a slim possibility that she had been right. For one thing, she herself sure had me fooled. I didn't suspect for one minute that she was running around on me. Until, of course, the day she left. I noticed it then.

Some detective I was.

Claudzilla came back to me, all lovey-dovey, right after she heard about the money Old Man Collins gave me for finding his granddaughter. Hard to believe, isn't it? Claudzilla looked me right in the eye and said she thought that we should get married again, that we should try to patch things up between us. She also happened to mention that this time around, she wanted a one-carat diamond wedding ring instead of "that cheap old thing" I gave her the last time.

Claudzilla threw her purse at me when I said no. I think that says it all.

I reckon Claudzilla has soured me on women some. I sure haven't dated much since we split up. Of course, it's not been entirely by my own choosing. Believe it or not, there are quite a few ladies out there who do not find the Howdy Doody type attractive.

I'm trying not to get cynical. I keep telling myself that there are still women in the world who aren't looking to pick a man's pocket, and that some of these non-pickpockets are actually in the market for a different kind of face than Tom Selleck's.

Who knows, maybe Cordelia could be one of these women. It could happen.

By the time I'd finished my dinner and given Rip the steak bone to gnaw on, I had convinced myself that Cordelia did so know she was accepting a date with me.

I went to sleep that night with a smile on my face.

CHAPTER

SEVEN

I was still smiling the next morning when I got up. What was not to be happy about? I had myself a date with Cordelia whether she knew it or not, and it was just hours away.

Also, it looked as though it were going to be a real nice autumn day, the air cool and crisp. I actually hummed a little to myself while I showered, got dressed, and made my breakfast.

Humming is not something I usually do, so Rip, naturally, followed me around, watching me real close, his brown eyes worried. "It's a beautiful day, okay?" I said, by way of explanation.

Rip looked at me suspiciously and cocked his head to one side. Obviously, my explanation didn't satisfy him. He still looked convinced that I'd gone nuts overnight. I ignored him and stayed cheerful.

Breakfast was my usual—frozen pancakes and bacon, both cooked in a matter of minutes in the microwave. There are folks who live down the road from me who still do their cooking on a wood stove. These folks—the Renfrows—also have a huge garden and a compost heap. I know about the compost heap because every once in a while, right after I've carried him down the steps, Rip will take off for a spell. If it's summer, Rip is likely as not to come back with decaying vegetables in his mouth. Which, of course, he scatters all over my yard. No doubt trying to do his part to make sure the grass gets enough fertilizer.

Me, I don't do compost. I also don't do any cooking on the wood stove I have in my living room. I only fire that thing up during the wintertime to help out the furnace. I mean, I like the idea of getting back to nature and a simpler life and all that, but I don't think there's any reason to go hog wild and give up all your modern conveniences.

I opened up the windows in my kitchen real wide, and took a deep breath. Just smelling that cool, fresh air made my microwaved pancakes and bacon taste even better. Even having to carry Rip up and down the steps before I left didn't ruin my mood.

In fact, I was still feeling pretty cheerful when I pulled up in front of Delbert Sims' place almost twenty minutes later. Delbert's house was right where Vergil had said it was. As I went down the gravel road in back of the Crayton County Supermarket, I passed a beat-up mailbox that said SIMS.

My good mood lasted right up until I got a load of Delbert's house. Actually, I use the term *house* only in the most general sense. *Dump* would probably describe it better.

This particular dump was made of stone just like the sheriff had told me, but those stones looked as if maybe some giant had picked them up and reshuffled them a little before he'd set them back down. The whole building seemed to lean a little.

I went up to the door. Badly in need of paint, and with one hinge off, the door looked as if a good wind might claim it at any moment. There was a rusty doorbell, but when I pushed it, nothing sounded inside. I pushed the doorbell a couple more times—apparently just for the fun of it—and then I gave up and knocked on the door.

On the fourth knock, Delbert opened the door. He was, to put it kindly, a mess. His black hair looked as if he hadn't washed it in a couple of months, and his face was gray with stubble. About my height, only at least thirty pounds heavier, he stood there at the door, swaying a little on his feet.

I wasn't surprised. There were those in Pigeon Fork who insisted that if Delbert Sims ever woke up completely sober, the shock might kill him.

Delbert was wearing a shirt and tie, believe it or not, and gray flannel slacks. Delbert, however, had gone in for the wrinkled look. And the one-sock-on, one-sock-off look. Sort of like Michael Jackson, only starting at your feet.

Delbert stared at me through bloodshot eyes. "What?" he said. I took a step back. His breath could've stopped a charging bull.

I'd seen Delbert on the street several times since I'd moved back to Pigeon Fork, and once—about two months ago—Pop Matheny had even introduced us. In his present condition, however, I wasn't sure Delbert would remember.

"I'm Haskell Blevins," I said. "I'm looking into the unfortunate death of Mrs. Turley, and I need to ask you a few questions."

Something flickered in Delbert's eyes. "What about?" he asked.

I smiled at him. Real calm. "Well, Delbert," I said

patiently, "if you'd let me come in a minute, I'll tell you."

Delbert eyed me suspiciously. "What would I wanna talk to you for?"

I smiled wider. "Because, if you don't talk to me, then I might just mention to Sheriff Minrath how real uncooperative you were. The sheriff just happens to be a close personal friend of mine. He might think you were being real unneighborly. *And* he might start wondering why."

Delbert mulled that one over. I stood there, watching him. Mulling, for Delbert, evidently involved wiping his nose on his sleeve, grunting, and scratching his protruding stomach. Finally, Delbert turned abruptly and walked away from the door.

I took that to mean, being as how Delbert wasn't blocking the door anymore, that I was welcome to come inside. Delbert was, no doubt, right up there with Emily Post as far as manners go.

I followed him inside with not a little trepidation. All the blinds and drapes were pulled, making it very dark inside Delbert's living room. Evidently, Delbert had some kind of problem with sunlight. Or maybe he had vampire friends staying with him.

Looking around, however, I immediately dismissed the thought. Even vampires wouldn't stoop this low.

No wonder Delbert didn't want any light in this room. If you pulled the drapes, you could see all too clearly what a pigsty this place was.

The more I looked around, though, the more I decided that calling this place a pigsty was unkind. Pigs wouldn't stoop this low, either.

There were empty beer cans scattered here and there on the floor, and three wadded-up potato chip bags on the sofa. On one end table was a glass half-filled with some dark brown liquid. On top of this liquid floated something that looked exactly like blue mold. Old magazines and newspapers littered the floor—a floor which, I might add, seemed a little on the gritty side when I walked across it.

I kept looking around that room, and—I admit it—I was impressed. Before I'd seen this place, I had thought my office was sloppy, but this was something else again. In the highly competitive world of sloppiness, Delbert had turned pro.

In one corner of the living room was a large philodendron which had evidently succumbed long ago to neglect. Covered with dust, the shriveled plant certainly added a decorator's touch to the room.

On the coffee table in the middle of the discolored rug was a congealed half-eaten pizza, heavy on the anchovies. No wonder Delbert's breath smelled like that. I was relieved. I'd begun to suspect that perhaps he'd died during the night, and that—in his inebriated condition—he'd forgotten to remain lying down.

Delbert was now slumped in one corner of the couch. He thoughtfully pushed the potato chip bags lying next to him onto the floor, and looked at me as if he actually expected me to sit down next to him.

I decided against it. There didn't seem to be a chance in a million that Delbert would be reaching for a breath mint anytime soon. I chose instead the brown Naugahyde recliner on the right of the sofa.

I immediately regretted my choice. As soon as I sat down, I noticed something. The arms of the recliner felt sticky. As if something like Coke—or beer—or, say, vomit—had been spilled on the recliner a long, long time ago, and left there to dry.

I certainly hoped it was either Coke or beer. What had made me think of that other choice was a faint smell that lingered in the room. I decided not to ask Delbert if he had any idea what that odor could be.

It was with a real effort, sitting stiffly in that recliner, that I managed to give old Delbert a smile. "Well now," I said, getting a Kleenex out of my pocket. I wiped my hands, then positioned them carefully in my lap, so that as few parts of me as possible were actually in touch with the recliner. "What can you tell me about the Friday night Mrs. Turley met her death?"

Delbert slumped a little more into the couch. His eyes seemed to glaze over for a minute. When they cleared, he said, "We were playing cards." He paused. "And she got killed."

I just looked at him. *Thank you, Delbert, for your play-by-play analysis of the night's events. What a big help.*

"Yes?" I asked.

Delbert nodded. "Yes," he said.

So much for trying to get Delbert to elaborate on his own.

"Who all was there?"

Delbert gave me a look. "Who do you think?" he asked.

That Delbert. He was the witty one.

"Well, besides you," I told him, "I'd say there was Grampap, Eunice, and Joe Eddy."

Delbert nodded again. "That's them."

I gave him another totally insincere smile. "And did anyone leave the room at any time during the evening?"

Delbert didn't answer for at least a minute. For a while there I thought maybe he'd nodded off. "Guess so," he finally said.

It went on like this for a while. I asked a question,

Delbert gave me a two-word answer. I asked another question, Delbert gave me another two-word answer. His account of the evening seemed to jibe with Joe Eddy's and Grampap's, but I was starting to think it would be easier to question Delbert's philodendron.

I'd just asked, "Then, you think that you might have left the room about three times that night?" when Delbert suddenly got to his feet.

"You want something to drink?" he said.

Somehow, I knew he wasn't talking about lemonade. I shook my head no, and Delbert ambled off into the kitchen. He came back with a glass of ice and an almost-full bottle of vodka. He sat down heavily on the sofa, filled the glass once, downed it, and filled it again. I could hardly watch him without my eyes watering.

Me, I can't stand vodka. I think it tastes like something you wash your toilet bowl with. Delbert, however, did not seem to have my reservations. He probably didn't wash his toilet bowl at all, and so he had no reason to make the comparison. Delbert smacked his lips over that first glass, burped noisily, and then looked back over at me. "Now what was you saying?"

It was the longest string of words I'd gotten out of him so far. After a couple of more glasses of vodka, though, Delbert began stringing together more and more words. By the time that vodka bottle was half empty, Delbert was talking up a storm.

"—and I don't unnerstan' why somebody woulda kilt poor Thelma. She was such a fine lady," Delbert blubbered. "Such a fine lady."

"Thelma?" I said.

Delbert gave me a watery stare. "Grammy's name was Thelma." He wiped at his eyes. "Don't know

why nobody never called her by her name no more."
He took another swig of vodka, this time not bothering to pour it in the glass first. Delbert evidently liked his vodka straight. Straight out of the bottle, straight into his stomach. "Everybody kept calling her Grammy," he whimpered. "Like she was a grandmother or something."

I decided not to point out to him that Mrs. Turley *was* a grandmother. Delbert didn't seem to be paying a whole lot of attention to me, anyway.

"Boy, oh, boy," he went on, "Thelma was looking real good that last night. Real good."

I remembered the flowered housedress and the terry cloth house shoes. Maybe when you're in your early sixties like Delbert here, your idea of what looks good on a woman changes a little. I nodded in Delbert's direction. "Thelma was one fine-looking woman," I said.

Delbert nodded back at me. "She come over that night, and she was a-sitting out there in the kitchen, a-talking to Eunice about her flower garden." Delbert took another swig of vodka. Straight again. I glanced away. "Eunice had just gotten the new catalogue from Harvee's Seed in the mail that day, and Thelma was looking so happy."

"Happy?" I said. "Why was she so happy?" Delbert was starting not to make a lot of sense.

He looked at me impatiently. " 'Cause Thelma hadn't gotten her own new Harvee's catalogue as yet, and Eunice was going to give Thelma hers."

Eunice hadn't mentioned anything about giving Grammy her catalogue. And, I was sure that the seed catalogue with Grammy's gardening stuff over at Grampap's had been last year's, not this year's. It probably wasn't anything, but I would have to remember to ask Eunice about it.

Delbert's voice was getting choked up now. "Poor Thelma spent her last night a-talking with Eunice about a garden she weren't never going to plant!" He wiped his eyes on his sleeve.

I thought about giving him my Kleenex, but it was the only one I had. And I was afraid that if I should accidentally touch the arm of the recliner again, I might need it.

"Do you have any idea who might have wanted to hurt Grammy?" I asked. "Or her pets?"

"Nope, I don't," Delbert said. He looked up at me, his eyes red-rimmed. "Ever'body loved Thelma. Ever'body surely did."

Delbert hadn't mentioned Grammy's pets. This seemed about as good a time as any to ask about them. "You know, Delbert," I said, "some folks around town think you're not any too crazy about animals. That they get on your nerves."

Delbert was not as drunk as I thought. Apparently, the man had developed a remarkable tolerance for the stuff over the years. His eyes suddenly focused and darted toward mine. "Hey now," he said, "I don't care what nobody says. I liked Thelma's pets. I really did." He looked around the room, as if searching for the right words. "Why, I thought that cat and that little bird were right cute."

This was a slight departure from the statement Delbert had given the police. Somehow, I didn't believe him. Particularly when the next thing out of his mouth was, "Besides, them pets even got on Thelma's nerves some of the time. You ask anybody. Them dang fool animals of hers got on ever'body's nerves some of the time. *Ever'body's.*" Delbert was warming to his subject now. "Dang cat was always jumping at your feet. And that bird was filthy. Just filthy."

Looking around us, I might've thought that particular trait would've given Delbert something in common with the bird. Something, perhaps, to bond them together in mutual understanding. Or some such.

Delbert was still ranting on. "Animals weren't meant to live with humans. They weren't. Else, why did God make them animals?"

So much for the cat and bird being cute. I was not about to get into a theological discussion with a drunk. I moved on to another topic. "Tell me," I said, leaning forward, "were you and Grammy ever engaged?"

Delbert's dull eyes brightened for about half a second. "It was a long time ago," he said. "Back in high school."

"What happened?" I asked.

Delbert just looked at me for a long moment. Evidently, though, the vodka was having an effect, after all. His glance eventually sort of slid away, and he looked as if he were about to cry. "I never should've let Thelma get away. Never should've," he said. "We belonged together."

I didn't say anything, but you would've thought from what Delbert said next, I'd argued with him. He looked me straight in the face, and said, "Oh, yes, it's true, all right. Thelma knew it, too. She knew we belonged together."

This was getting interesting. "She did?" I said.

Delbert waved his bottle at me. "You don' believe me, but it's true. Thelma told me that last week that Grampap was getting on her nerves. That she was sick of him." Delbert nodded his head at me, like a little kid trying to convince an adult he was telling the truth. "Oh, yes, she did," he said. "She really did."

"Was she going to leave Grampap for you?" I asked.

Delbert looked away. "She never came right out and said it. She was too much of a lady for that. But I knew. I knew that's what she was a-going to do."

"When did she tell you all this?" I asked. If what Delbert was saying were true, it gave Grampap a motive for murder even bigger than a satellite dish. Lord, was such a thing possible? Could that little old man really have murdered his wife *and* her pets?

"It was a couple of days before she died," Delbert said. "I called her up on the phone—just like I did sometimes. To keep in touch, you know." He looked over at me, slyly. Somehow, the idea of Delbert "keeping in touch" with any woman was not a welcome thought. Still, Grammy had known him long before he fell in love with the bottle. Maybe she saw a Delbert I didn't see.

She would've had to.

Delbert leaned my way, and said in a low, confidential voice, "Me and Grammy stayed close over the years. We did. We had us a real special relationship. *Real* special." His eyes teared up. Delbert blinked a couple of times, and wiped his nose on his sleeve.

I don't know how Grammy could've resisted that kind of charm.

I had one more question. "Did Grammy—uh, Thelma—ever mention some folks by the name of Myrldean Bleemel or Ray Don Peters?"

Delbert gave me a hard stare. As hard as he could, considering his eyes were so bleary. "Sure did," he said. "What about 'em?"

"That's what I'm asking you," I said. Slowly and distinctly. "What about them?"

Delbert took another sip, and then shrugged his shoulders. "She hated their guts."

This was not anything like the response I'd been

expecting. My mouth almost dropped open. "What do you mean?"

Delbert looked at me as if maybe I was the one who'd just put away half a bottle of vodka. *"She hated their guts,"* he said, emphasizing every word.

Right. I understood that part. Thank you, Delbert, for clearing that up for me. "What I meant to ask was—why?" I said. I think I was showing remarkable patience here.

Delbert shrugged again. "Well, Myrldean was a bitch. Always making fun of Thelma behind her back. And Ray Don—he was an asshole."

Well, now, that did seem to explain everything. "Did Grammy tell you she hated them?" I asked.

Delbert gave me another one of them "Are you drunk?" looks. "How else would I know?"

Something else seemed suddenly to occur to him, and Delbert leaned unsteadily toward me. Remembering his lack of breath mints, I leaned back.

"They're both dead, you know," Delbert whispered.

Thanks again, Delbert. Tell me something I don't know. "You don't say," I said.

Delbert nodded his head, his bleary eyes wide. "Ray Don broke his neck, falling down his basement steps. And Myrldean fell and cracked her head on the sidewalk. A long time ago." It didn't seem to be breaking Delbert's heart to recount their deaths.

"Did you know these two people, too?" I asked.

Delbert looked over at me, as if measuring my words. I couldn't tell if Delbert's natural demeanor was one of acting suspicious—or if he was just one of those guys who always looked guilty regardless.

"Sure I knew them," Delbert said. His tone was defensive. "I used to work with Ray Don. We both took early retirement from the lumber mill a year ago.

And Myrldean went to the same church as me and Grammy."

Delbert leaned back on the couch, and added, "Yep, I knew 'em all right, but I didn't hate neither one of them as bad as Grammy did." Delbert seemed to think this was a real plus in his favor.

"What made Ray Don such an asshole?" It seemed a reasonable thing to want to know. Probably, even Ray Don himself might've asked the same thing.

Delbert had an immediate answer. "Ray Don thought he was a Don Juan." Delbert pronounced the name, Don Jew-wan, but I knew what he meant. "And he was always bragging," Delbert added. "Ray Don was always saying his flower garden was better'n Thelma's. It got on her nerves."

According to Delbert, Grammy's nerves must've been completely trampled, what with Grampap, the cat, the bird, Myrldean and now, Ray Don, all getting on them. In fact, it seemed as if Delbert himself was the only person who didn't get on Grammy's nerves. Watching Delbert down more vodka, I found it hard to believe. I also wondered if Delbert knew what he was talking about.

I had just one more question. "By the way," I said, "now that the Friday-night Rook game has broken up, do you see much of Joe Eddy or Grampap anymore?"

Delbert's eyes suddenly narrowed, and for a second, he looked stone-cold sober. "Nope, I don't," he said.

"You don't?" I said. "You don't see them at all?" This was kind of a surprise.

"Nope, I don't." Delbert seemed a little agitated now.

"Really?" I said.

"Look, I said I didn't see them," Delbert said shortly. He seemed real irritated for some reason.

He abruptly got to his feet. Any idea that he could've been sober immediately vanished. Weaving badly, he waved the vodka bottle at me. "Look, I'm tired." He started moving toward me and eyeing the front door over my shoulder. "Uh, I don't feel like answering no more stupid questions, unnerstan'?"

I understood. I'm quick. I pick up real fast on this kind of subtle nuance.

On my way out the door, I didn't bother to thank Delbert for his help. He probably wouldn't have remembered it, anyway.

It didn't take five minutes for me to get back to my office. I spent that five minutes wondering what had suddenly put a burr in old Delbert's saddle. Why did my just mentioning his old Rook partners make him suddenly so irritated?

Driving back into town, I decided not to park in the alley again. I parked my truck right out in front of Elmo's Drugstore, so that if the Pigeon Fork Tire Slasher felt at all inclined to strike again, he'd have to do it in front of the entire town.

I hadn't climbed two steps before I heard it. My phone was ringing. And ringing. And ringing.

Melba was doing her usual good job.

CHAPTER
EIGHT

I took the stairs to my office two at a time, all the while cursing Melba. And wondering whether I'd made her mad, telling her I didn't need her help questioning folks. Maybe I should've been a little more diplomatic.

I was also wondering whether I should connect up my answering machine again. I had myself an answering machine the first week or so after I opened up my agency. It worked real good, picking up calls on the third ring. In fact, there was only one problem that I had with it. Nobody who called me would leave me a message.

All I got recorded on the thing was a whole lot of hang-ups. And a couple of these: "Hey, come here, listen to this—it's one of them there answering thing-amabobs!" And then, naturally, hooting and laughing.

It seemed to take forever to get the door to my office open, what with the phone ringing off its hook inside. Once I was in, I bumped into the same lamp I'd hit when Cordelia was here. I have got to remember to move that lamp. Or, maybe, throw it out. It had to be on at least the fifth or sixth ring that I finally grabbed up the receiver.

For a second, I thought whoever it was had hung up, or that something had gone wrong with my phone. I couldn't hear anything on the line except a loud, wailing sound. Then, finally, I heard the words, "Oh Haskell." Once that was said, however, there was only more wailing. And weeping. And sobbing.

I couldn't make out who it was. "Yes?" I said. It was a woman, I was reasonably sure. Being as how I didn't know too many men who would call me up crying and carrying on.

"Oh, it's awful! Oh, Lordy, Lordy, Lordy. It's awful!" Now, in addition to the weeping and wailing, there was a kind of hiccupping on the line. For a second I thought it was something else wrong with the connection, but then I realized it was my caller doing the hiccupping. In between the wails. And the sobs.

I may be cold-hearted, but this was starting to get old. "What exactly is awful?" I asked.

Whoever it was on the other end seemed to get a hold of herself a little. She hiccupped only a couple of more times, and then she took a deep breath. "Fluffy's been killed!" she said.

Her voice was ragged, but I knew then, of course, exactly who I was talking to. I can't say that I was overjoyed to hear from her.

"You got to get over here," she wailed on, "right this minute!"

Actually, it was about ten minutes later that I pulled up to Emmaline Johnston's house. It was situated right on the edge of town, a small brick ranch with a neat white picket fence running all around the yard.

The nearest house, however, was a good two blocks away. When I got out of my truck and saw Emmaline's yard, I understood why. Her neighbors probably wouldn't let her get any closer.

Emmaline's yard was filled to overflowing with lawn creatures. There were brightly painted ducks and geese and cardinal birds, all made of plywood, all with colorful wings that spun around and around every time there was a breeze. There were also frogs and turtles—with legs that spun—and even what looked to be a little Dutchboy. His arms spun around.

A pretty good wind was blowing when I walked up to Emmaline's front door. Watching all that commotion going on—all those spinning arms and wings and legs—made you feel a little strange. All those creatures seemed to be frantically signaling for help. Or maybe trying to warn you about something.

I had just lifted my hand to knock on Emmaline's door, trying to ignore what was going on out in her yard, when the door was flung open. *"There* you are!" she sobbed. "Thank God you're here!"

Emmaline was wearing a pink-and-white robe with ruffles on the front and ruffles at the sleeves. I noticed because all those ruffles made her look even larger as she hurled herself at my chest.

There didn't seem anything else to do but catch her.

For a woman in her fifties, Emmaline was built pretty solid. Having her fling herself at me was like being tackled by a fullback. If I'd known it was coming, I could've braced myself. As it was, when she hit me I staggered backward, and it was only by a monumental effort that I managed to regain my balance.

I fact, I came real close to landing smack-dab in the

middle of all those lawn creatures. Or maybe being impaled on one. With Emmaline on top of me.

That would not have been a pretty picture. Maybe this was what all those creatures out in her yard had been trying to warn me about.

Once I had my balance back, Emmaline hung onto my shoulders, sobbing away, for a good long while. Longer than I thought was absolutely necessary. I was sure she wouldn't cry this much if, say, *I* ever got murdered.

Emmaline still had the same tortoiseshell glasses hanging by the same black rope hanging around her neck as she'd worn in my office earlier. I noticed this because, while she pressed herself against me, sobbing, those glasses were digging their way painfully into my chest.

I squirmed and patted Emmaline's back. "There, there," I said. I don't know what that means, but it's what everybody seems to say in situations like this.

When the front of my shirt seemed to be sufficiently moistened, Emmaline pulled away. "I'm so sorry," she said, running her hand along the side of her head. Her French twist did look the worse for wear. It looked as if it had been knocked to one side, and several strands of black hair had escaped the twist part in the back. These strands stuck out at odd angles on both sides of Emmaline's head, giving her a slightly punk look. "I—I just can't believe he's gone! He was so young!"

I didn't know what to say to that. If you think I don't know what to say when a human dies, imagine how great I am with pets. I contented myself with just shaking my head and looking mournful, as I followed Emmaline inside, rubbing my chest.

Emmaline's furniture was Early American, but her overall decorating scheme was Cat. There were cats curled up on the sofa, cats sitting on the bookcases, cats lounging on top of the TV. Emmaline seemed to have ever kind of cat I could think of. Tabbies, Persians, Siamese, alley cats—even one without a tail. I looked around and wondered how on earth she even noticed one was missing.

Where there wasn't a real live cat, Emmaline had ceramic cats and kittens. On end tables, on the coffee table, and on a curio shelf on one wall. Above her TV Emmaline had what looked to be a family portrait. Twelve feline faces looked out at you, each cat face framed by a gray linen oval mat. I glanced at the portrait, and wondered which one was Fluffy.

As soon as I walked into the living room, all the cats in there looked up from whatever they were doing and watched me. A couple of them flicked their tails in my direction and walked regally out of the room, out into the hall. The rest just stared.

I suddenly knew what a mouse must feel like.

I also noticed something else the second I walked through the door. Emmaline had said it was difficult keeping her litter boxes clean for all those cats. Apparently, the situation had reached crisis proportions. My eyes started watering real bad. I blinked a couple of times, and started watching real careful where I stepped.

"He—he's in here," Emmaline said in a broken voice, leading the way to the bathroom. I followed her. It was a good thing I was watching where I stepped because a gray tabby and a Siamese followed me, walking precariously close to my feet.

Emmaline opened her bathroom door, and then

stood aside to let me pass. Her bathroom was done in aqua—aqua shower curtain, aqua tiles, aqua fixtures. If it wasn't the ugliest bathroom I'd ever seen, it was right up there in the top five. The wallpaper had tiny aqua kittens jumping across it. Emmaline must've looked high and low to find that particular pattern. And to find the three ceramic aqua cat plaques that hung above her aqua towels.

Emmaline moved aside, narrowly missing the Siamese that had followed me in. "Poor Fluffy. Poor, poor baby," she said, wiping her eyes. They needed wiping. Long streaks of mascara had made their way down each of her cheeks. "He—he's behind there," she added, pointing at the aqua shower curtain.

I pulled the curtain aside, and sure enough, there was a big, white Persian lying on its side in the aqua bathtub. It looked like one of those big, furry, stuffed toy cats folks used to put on top of their bed. This one, however, didn't look in any too great a condition. Its mouth was slightly open, and its eyes were fixed and staring. Fluffy apparently had met his death looking very shocked and terribly disappointed.

I swallowed, then reached out and touched the cat very tentatively. Just as I thought. Old Fluff was stiff as a board.

The Siamese who'd followed me in now hopped up on the edge of the tub, watching me. I picked him up and petted him absently while I looked around. The window above the tub was half open. I leaned forward to look out.

Behind me, Emmaline said, "See? Do you see it? Somebody cut the screen."

I had already seen it before she'd spoken. You would've had to be blind not to notice that an L had been sliced in the wire, so that now the screen hung open like a flap. On the inside window sill right in front of the flap was a small mound of hamburger. It looked as if some of the mound had been eaten.

"*I* never gave Fluffy hamburger," Emmaline said. "I always feed my babies Catty Cuisine cat food— never, *never* table scraps." Her tone implied that cats were too good to eat the same food that we humans eat.

I decided not to discuss that with her. "When did you find him?" I asked.

"As soon as I got up." In back of me, I could tell Emmaline was gearing up for some major wailing again. I recognized the hiccups from our telephone conversation earlier.

I tried to head her off. "Did you hear anything suspicious outside last night?" I was no cat coroner, but as stiff as he was, Fluffy must've been dead a while. Not to mention, the color and smell of the hamburger. It had been on that window sill for some time.

Emmaline shook her head, blinking back tears. "I didn't hear anything. It could've happened anytime during the night." She turned tortured eyes to mine. "Fluffy spent all his nights sitting in the bathroom window. Ever since I stopped letting him out at sunset." She swallowed noisily, and then added, "He took it real hard, his not being able to go out. He'd sit there for hours, looking out the window."

Emmaline looked at me as if expecting me to say something to that. Once again, I scrambled in my mind for the right response. I settled for just shaking my head again mournfully. That didn't seem to be enough, though. Emmaline was still looking at me expectantly. "Poor Fluffy," I added.

Emmaline nodded, satisfied. "Poor Fluffy," she agreed, her voice shaking. She wiped her eyes again, and added, "Whoever did this must've seen Fluffy sitting there, and—and—and—"

It was like listening to a stuck record. I held up my hand. "Have you reported this to the sheriff?"

Emmaline gave up trying to finish her other sentence, and just shook her head. "I bet the sheriff won't even come over here. I bet he'll think this is nothing." Her eyes were threatening to spill over again.

"He'll come over," I said real quick, hoping to head off the waterworks. "Matter of fact, I think he'll be real interested."

"Real interested" was probably a slight exaggeration, but Vergil did show up. It took him about an hour, but eventually he came walking up to Emmaline's front door, his eyes watching what all was going on in her front yard worriedly.

I couldn't help but notice that Emmaline did not tackle Vergil the minute she saw *him*. Maybe it pays to walk around frowning all the time.

I also noticed that my slashed tires rated Vergil *and* a deputy, whereas Fluffy only rated Vergil. I did not point this out to Emmaline, however. She had enough to grieve about as it was.

Vergil scooped up the hamburger out of the bathroom window and put it in one of the evidence bags he always seemed to have on hand. "No doubt in my mind that the lab is going to find out this is poisoned." He actually said this as if maybe Emmaline and I hadn't figured it out yet. I tried to looked impressed at his amazing deductive powers.

After that, Vergil went on back into the living room,

dodging cats, to take Emmaline's statement. It took hours. Of course, one reason it took so long was that Emmaline took time out every so often to do her wailing and hiccupping.

The whole time he was taking Emmaline's statement, Vergil looked just as though he were at a funeral. Emmaline, however, seemed to interpret this as an appropriate response to Fluffy's passing. I wasn't about to remind her that Vergil always looked like this.

While Vergil was occupied with Emmaline, I walked outside, around back. I wasn't really sure what I was looking for. A note maybe. Something.

There wasn't anything I could see, though. The grass under the bathroom window was beaten down a bit, but the ground was too dry to leave any footprints.

I was a little surprised at there not being a note. You'd think the killer would've wanted to rub it in. Of course, maybe his hands were full, what with having to carry around ground beef and poison and wire cutters. There might not have been any room for a pencil and paper.

A while later, when Vergil was finally ready to leave, he took me aside. "So, what do you think, Haskell?" he asked, brushing cat hair off the front of his slacks. He looked a tad irritated. "Do you think this has anything to do with the Turley case?"

I nodded. "Sure do," I said. "She did get all those notes. It looks like whoever it was made good on his threats."

The sheriff looked doubtful. "I don't know. There wasn't a note this time. And, let's face it, there's a whole lot of folks in this world who hate cats. And some, right here in Pigeon Fork, who especially hate *Emmaline's* cats.'' He picked another cat hair off his sleeve. I was pretty sure by then that Vergil could be numbered among this last group. Hell, he could probably be the group's leader.

Vergil didn't say anything else for a minute, but I knew what he was thinking. There were also probably quite a few folks right here in Pigeon Fork who not only couldn't stand her cats, but also couldn't stand Emmaline. And, if you happened to want to hurt Emmaline, the best way you could do it was to put a hit on one of her cats.

Fluffy had obviously been poisoned by somebody who'd come over to Emmaline's house with just that purpose in mind. I don't think anybody runs around with raw hamburger, poison, and wire cutters in their pocket, just in case. Also, whoever it was had known that Emmaline wasn't letting her cats out anymore— and that he'd need to bring along some tools to break in.

The killer had probably gone around the house, seen the cat in the bathroom window, and Fluffy's fate had been sealed.

Vergil was scratching his bald spot again. "But why now? Emmaline's been writing her letters to the editor for months. Why would whoever it is decide to kill one of her cats now?''

I didn't have the answer to that one. "Maybe he just ran out of patience. It does seem like too much of a coincidence, though, that somebody would just happen to kill one of Emmaline's cats—and it *not* be the person who wrote her all those threatening letters,'' I said.

The sheriff nodded. "I reckon so.''

117

"And," I went on, "I'd be real surprised if whoever wrote those notes was not involved in the Turley murder."

Vergil sighed. He is real good at sighing. I think I've mentioned this already. "I guess I'll be sending somebody over here to dust for fingerprints," he said. "And I'm going to do me some talking to Delbert Sims again. Far as I can tell, he's on the top of my list. I reckon I'll see what Delbert's been up to lately."

I decided not to tell him I'd just talked to Delbert myself. Maybe having the sheriff drop in on him might do Delbert good. Soften him up a bit. So that if he were involved in this, Delbert might do something stupid and give himself away.

Vergil told Emmaline to expect somebody to come by to dust for fingerprints, and then he walked slowly around the house twice. He didn't seem to find anything more than I did, but as I watched him leave— still brushing off cat hairs with an air of genuine sadness—I had a feeling things were going to get real interesting real soon.

Emmaline, however, didn't seem at all impressed with Vergil. She came up beside me and watched the sheriff getting into his car. "He'll never catch who did this," she said. "It's up to you, Haskell. You have got to stop this maniac before he kills again!"

She was working herself up again. "I'll do my best," I said. "In the meantime, if I were you, I'd keep all my windows and doors locked."

Emmaline's eyes got real big at that.

"Just to be on the safe side, okay?" I added.

"Oh. Sure," she said, her eyes looking worriedly back at her house. Poor thing. Emmaline looked very vulnerable suddenly.

118

"You'll be okay," I said, trying to sound a lot more sure of it than I was.

Emmaline twisted the Kleenex she was holding. "I know I will," she said. Her eyes said something else. "Besides, I've learnt my lesson. I'm not never, never, never going to write any more letters. Nosirree-bob."

That seemed a good course of action. Lord knows, whoever killed Fluffy would be pleased. It kind of made me mad that doing what he did had worked. But I sure didn't blame Emmaline.

I offered to bury Fluffy for her, but Emmaline wouldn't hear of it. "I'll be taking him on over to the funeral home," she said. Her tone implied that I should have known that.

Of course. I tried to look as if that didn't surprise me one bit. Didn't everybody have their pets buried by a funeral home? "I'm sure they'll give Fluffy a fine burial," I said, feeling like an idiot to even be saying such a thing.

Emmaline looked at me as if she would've agreed with the idiot assessment. "Oh, no," she said. Her tone was haughty. "I'm going to have Fluffy cremated."

I tried to hold my face real still, afraid that if my face chose an expression of its own free will, it might choose laughing out loud. "Well, of course," I said. "What was I thinking of?" Emmaline was probably planning to scatter Fluffy's ashes over a field of catnip.

I was close. "I'm going to mix Fluffy's ashes with catnip," Emmaline went on, "and I'm going to keep them in an urn on my mantle."

I didn't even blink. "What a good idea," I said.

I needed to get out of there.

It was getting real close to time to pick up Cordelia,

anyway. If I hurried, I'd just have time to shower and change. I sure didn't want to show up on Cordelia's doorstep smelling like Essence of Litter Box.

I made my way out to the truck. The wind had died down by then, so Emmaline's lawn creatures had calmed down. All of them just seemed to be waving lazily in the breeze.

Emmaline stood at her door and waved, too. "Thank you for coming," she said.

I did feel kind of sorry for her. They say people who are real crazy about animals have turned to them for company because their fellow humans have hurt them so badly. Emmaline must've been tortured as a child.

I drove on home, carried Rip up and down the steps, and started getting ready to leave. Rip figured out a long time ago that if I take a shower at night, it means I'll be going back out again. So he kept barking at me off and on, the whole time I was getting ready. Sitting there just outside of the bathroom, barking. And looking at me accusingly.

Rip is a lot like a wife in this respect. In every bark you could hear: *You've left me alone here all day, and now you're going out again. I've given you the best years of my life, and this is the thanks I get.*

I think Rip picked up this routine from my ex-wife. He spent the formative years of his life back in Louisville living with me and Claudzilla. Claudzilla was the world's champion pouter—she'd start in the second she realized I was going out in the evening without her. No matter what the reason. Whether it was doing surveillance, or meeting with the chief of police, or anything. Claudzilla pouted, just like Rip.

Unlike your wife, though, you can just ignore your dog. I gave Rip a dog treat—one of those dried beef strips that look about as appetizing as the bottom of your shoe—and I went on out the door.

Rip picked up the beef strip and followed me out to the deck. I half expected him to throw the beef strip at me—that's what Claudzilla would've done. But all Rip did was sit down and start gnawing on the thing. He didn't even look up when I went down the driveway.

Claudzilla could still teach him a thing or two.

CHAPTER

NINE

Cordelia was sure looking pretty. She was sitting out on the porch swing in front of Robey's Boarding House when I pulled up. It made me feel kind of proud, knowing a woman that looked like this was actually waiting for me.

Cordelia was wearing a black flowered dress made of some kind of filmy fabric, and she had a black beaded sweater draped around her shoulders.

Even though it was September, it was still getting real warm during the day. The evenings, though, were starting to get kind of chilly. I wondered if that sweater was going to be enough. I decided not to mention it, though. Maybe Cordelia would get so cold, she would want us to huddle together to keep warm. The thought was enough to make me smile real big as I got out of my truck.

"You sure look as if you're in a good mood," Cordelia said, getting up and coming over to meet me.

How could I be in anything other than a good mood

122

looking at her? I actually considered saying that to her, but I was afraid it would sound like a line she'd probably heard a million times before.

I ended up saying instead, "As a matter of fact, I am in a good mood." And then grinning at her like some geek. Do I have a way with women or what?

Cordelia, however, didn't seem to notice what a geek I was. She just gave me another one of her dazzling smiles, and then she did an even more wonderful thing. She looked over at my truck, and her smile didn't dim.

What a woman.

Now, this may sound like an insignificant thing, but you'd be surprised how many women blanche when they realize you're actually going to take them out in a truck. There are fewer of this particular type of woman around these parts—being as how their options sometimes dwindle down to two: Either you go with a guy in a truck, or you don't go out. But, believe it or not, there are still a lot of women in Pigeon Fork who choose the latter—and loudly voice that choice.

In the four months I've been back here in Pigeon Fork, I've gone out with just two women. One blancher, and one non-blancher. The non-blancher I kept on seeing for a while until I finally had to face facts. She was real cute and all, but there were doorknobs in Pigeon Fork with more smarts. And while brains is not one of my primary requirements in a woman, being able to talk in complete sentences is. I guess I'm just picky that way.

Cordelia did seem to be able to put nouns and verbs together. For example, when she got into my truck, she said, looking around at the leather interior, "My goodness, this is nice."

Right away she had my last date beat bad in the vocabulary department.

I really couldn't smile at Cordelia enough. Her short brown hair was pulled back on each side with tortoiseshell barrettes, and it hung in glossy curls around her oval face. She was wearing something on her lips that made them look very red, very shiny, and very kissable. "So, where are we going for dinner?" she asked.

It wasn't as if there were any big choice. There is only one real nice place to eat anywhere near here. Gentry's Family Restaurant. Actually, Gentry's isn't really in Pigeon Fork—it's about ten miles outside of town, traveling north on the interstate.

The restaurant itself is only a sideline for the Gentry family. Mainly, what the Gentrys do is run their U-Pick-Em Farm, getting people to come from as far away as Louisville to stand in the Gentry fields and sweat buckets picking strawberries and tomatoes and assorted vegetables.

You can buy prepicked strawberries and tomatoes and assorted vegetables for a few cents more per pound at Gentry's Market, located right next door to their restaurant. This is what folks from Pigeon Fork always do. But the people from out of town who could no doubt well afford the few extra cents? These are the ones that seem to feel that standing in the hot sun for a few hours to save a couple of pennies makes real good sense.

As I said before, go figure.

The U-Pick-Em Farm starts winding down, though, in September. There're still some pumpkins and a little broccoli and maybe some spinach, but there isn't anywhere near what there is during the warmer months.

The colder it gets, the more the Gentrys concentrate on the restaurant end of the business. You can tell it, too. In the summer Mama Gentry might be a mite snippity with you when you stop by to eat, acting as though maybe you interrupted her day. In the autumn and winter, though, she's always real nice, beaming at you the minute you walk in the door.

She was there at the door when Cordelia and I walked in, smiling and nodding at us like one of them ceramic dogs folks used to have in the back window of their car. Cordelia and I nodded and smiled right back at Mama Gentry as we made our way to one of the tables next to the windows.

At Gentry's you don't wait at the entrance to be shown to your table. You just go ahead and get yourself one. In fact, if you try to stand there and wait for Mama Gentry or one of her kids to show you to a table, you'll really irritate the people piling up behind you.

Not to mention how irritated Mama Gentry will get. She's one of them big-boned, heavyset farm women, too. She looks as if she could hurt you bad. And, judging from the expression on her face sometimes, she'd enjoy it.

Cordelia sat down in the chair facing the rest of the room—the chair I usually like to get. This time I really didn't mind, though, because Cordelia was the only thing I wanted to look at. She leaned against the back of the chair, smoothing her skirt and looking around approvingly. "This looks very nice," she said. The dining room *is* real cheerful with its red-and-white-checkered tablecloths and its red plastic flowers in white vases on every table.

I could tell right away that Cordelia had class. She picked up the red paper napkin that lay folded at the side of her plate, and she put it in her lap. I was impressed. My last date stuck a corner of her napkin in the neck of her dress, like a bib. Of course, as it turned out, she needed a bib.

Once the napkin was on her lap, though, Cordelia seemed sort of at a loss. She kept looking around the room, then down at the table, then back at me. It took me a minute to realize what it was she was waiting for. A menu.

Gentry's doesn't exactly have menus. The meals are served family style, meaning they just bring you a bunch of bowls of food, and you help yourself. The side dishes are always the same—corn on the cob, green beans, lima beans, mashed potatoes, and biscuits.

The only thing that changes is the main dish, and Gentry's has thoughtfully printed your choices on the paper placemat under each plate. Folks from around here don't even look at it, since the selection is always the same thing every single night. Fried chicken, pork chops, fried steak, or fish.

I read somewhere that you can always tell an American in a restaurant in Europe because of how we cut our meat. I think it has something to do with the way we switch forks from one hand to the other or something like that. In Pigeon Fork you can always tell somebody from out of town because they're the only ones who are lifting up their plates in Gentry's Restaurant so they can read the menu.

"The menu is printed on your placemat," I told Cordelia, keeping my voice low, "but I can tell you what your choices are." I started naming them off, but evidently Cordelia needed documentation. She had her plate in the air before I'd even gotten to "pork chops." I noticed a couple of folks in the dining room nod in Cordelia's direction and snicker.

People can be so cruel.

After we gave one of the Gentry daughters our order—both of us went with the fried chicken, a sign of true compatibility, I thought—Cordelia started pumping me for what I'd found out from Delbert Sims.

I had hoped we could've started on a more personal note, but what the hey, at least I was sitting opposite a really pretty woman whose attention, for the moment, was totally focused on me.

I went over Delbert's account of the night Grammy died, noting all the while how truly gorgeous Cordelia's eyes were. I told her how his story pretty much matched up with everybody else's, and I finished up by saying, "Delbert also confirmed something I'd already heard—apparently he was engaged to Grammy at one time."

Cordelia looked surprised. "Really?" she said. She shook her head in disbelief. "I guess I never thought of Grammy with anybody other than Grampap." She smiled fondly. "They were always so cute together."

I decided there wasn't any use in telling her what Delbert had said about Grammy still being interested in him. The old guy was probably just wishing out loud, anyway.

"When is the last time you saw Grammy and Grampap together?" I asked.

Cordelia shrugged. "This last Christmas." Her eyes teared up some, and she went on in a shaky voice, "I came down here with my husband Christmas week. Just for a visit. Eunice and Joe Eddy and all of us got together at Grammy's for Christmas dinner. It—it was so nice."

I tried to follow what she was saying, but if the truth be known, the last thing I really heard was one word. *Husband*. My mouth actually went dry. Cordelia had said "husband." In fact, what she'd said was, "*my* husband." That was worse.

Up to that moment, it hadn't occurred to me that Cordelia could possibly be married. For one thing her name was still Turley. But, maybe, Cordelia was one of them modern-type women who don't change their names anymore when they get themselves married.

I always thought that was a dirty trick.

I guess I should've known Cordelia was taken. How could a woman like her walk around unmarried? Only in a world of blind men. I hoped I didn't look as totally disappointed as I felt.

"I guess I would've gotten back here sooner," Cordelia was going on, "but then I started going through the divorce right after that, and what with trying to get myself established in a new apartment and all—"

Cordelia went on, but I had lost the thread again. My heart skipped a beat. She was divorced! *Divorced!* Wasn't that wonderful?

Or was it? Why would any man in his right mind leave a woman like Cordelia? I wanted real bad to ask, but how do you bring something up like that? Oh, by the way, were you impossible to live with—or was he?

I guess, even if you could ask, there'd be no way you'd get a straight answer, anyway. Who in the world was going to admit: *Why, yes, now that you mention it, I made his life a living hell, and he finally had the good sense to run screaming.*

There was no doubt in my mind that even as Cordelia and I were talking, my ex-wife Claudzilla was out on a date somewhere, saying all sorts of terribly unflattering things about me. Her date probably didn't even have to ask. Claudzilla would volunteer the information. She was probably telling some poor schnook right this minute that Rip and I had an unnatural relationship.

"—but Grammy and I still kept in touch," Cordelia was saying. "Through letters. I guess we wrote each other about every three weeks or so."

I nodded. "When was the last time you heard from her?"

I almost wished I hadn't asked. Cordelia's blue eyes swam with unshed tears again. "It—it was just two weeks before."

I knew very well what she meant by "before."

"Did Grammy say anything unusual in that last letter? Anything that might have struck you as odd?"

Mama Gentry picked that moment to bring us over a basketful of homemade bread and carrots and crackers. The large woman gave me and Cordelia a toothy grin as she turned to leave. I smiled back at her. I reckon I've always been a little afraid not to return Mama Gentry's smile.

Cordelia took a bite of a carrot stick, blinking tears away, before she answered. "Well, now that you mention it," she said, "Grammy was complaining about a friend of hers—Ray Don Something or another."

I buttered a slice of bread and started eating it. Ray Don Peters again. His name did seem to keep coming up. "What did Grammy say about him?"

"She said he was being a royal pain. That he was bragging to the whole town that his garden was prettier than hers. You know, stuff like that."

Vergil had told me that Ray Don had departed this earth about a year ago. So, as best as I could figure, Ray Don would've been dead almost five months by the time Grammy wrote that letter. I was just thinking that maybe it might be a good idea to talk to Ray Don Peters' neighbors when Cordelia leaned forward. "Say, do you think this Ray Don person could've been the one who—who—?"

I shook my head. "I doubt it."

Cordelia was not convinced. "But, Haskell," she said, pointing her carrot stick at me, "maybe Ray Don went crazy, and wanted to make sure his garden was the best or something, and he—"

"I really don't think Ray Don could possibly have done it," I said.

"But, Haskell—"

So I had to tell her. Once I explained the situation, Cordelia had to admit that Ray Don could probably be scratched off the list of possible suspects.

As the implication of all this dawned on her, Cordelia's big blue eyes got even bigger. "Oh, dear," she said. She looked down at her lap for a second, and then back up at me, and then down at her lap again. Then she took a big bite out of her carrot stick and chewed it real slow.

"Well," Cordelia finally said, her eyes defiant, "this doesn't mean anything, really. Grammy was still all right, she was just a little forgetful, that's all."

Right. And Hitler was just a little rude. I just looked at her.

Cordelia practically glared back at me. For some reason, she seemed suddenly indignant. "There wasn't anything really wrong with Grammy," she said stubbornly. "She just forgot things every once in a while. Grammy was still OK."

"Of course, she was," I said. Anybody could forget that a friend of theirs was dead. It happened all the time.

I wasn't about to spend the evening arguing about just how crazy Grammy really was. What difference did it make, anyway? The last thing I wanted was Cordelia getting mad at *me* because her grandmother might have been a little on the batty side.

"I don't guess Grammy was any worse than anybody else her age," I added. I didn't really believe it, but as they say, once you can fake sincerity, you've got it made.

Apparently, I could fake sincerity pretty good because Cordelia gave me a sheepish little smile, and said, "I guess I am a little sensitive about this. But I don't want horrible rumors spreading about Grammy, you know? I mean, Grammy would turn over in her grave, if something like this were being whispered about her." Her smile grew wider. "We Turleys are real proud, you know."

I smiled back at her, but something about the way Cordelia said all that bothered me. She sounded just like Eunice on the phone last night. In fact, Eunice had used almost the exact same words. Grammy was real proud, Eunice had said.

I got myself a carrot stick, and took a bite. "By the way," I said, "have you talked to Eunice lately?"

Cordelia looked happy to be talking about something other than Grammy's peculiarities. "As a matter of fact, I have," she said. "I talked to Eunice last night right after I phoned you. She called up wanting to know how the investigation was going." Cordelia ate the last of her carrot stick, and reached for another one. "You know, Joe Eddy and Eunice are real concerned. They're every bit as anxious as I am that Grammy's killer be brought to justice."

Eunice, maybe. But Joe Eddy? I doubted if Joe Eddy would care if Jack the Ripper was brought to justice.

"What all did you tell Eunice?"

Cordelia picked up another carrot. "Oh, just about everything you told me," she said. "Eunice seemed real interested."

I made my voice real casual. "I bet you even told her about Emmaline's trouble with all her cats."

Cordelia smiled. "I sure did. Eunice thought it was kinda funny, poor Emmaline having to keep all her cats indoors."

I bet Joe Eddy thought it was real amusing, too. I wondered if he hadn't put Eunice up to calling Cordelia. "It turns out Emmaline was right to be worried," I said.

Cordelia looked at me questioningly.

I nodded. "Somebody killed one of Emmaline's cats last night."

Cordelia's hand went to her throat. "Oh, my," she said. "That's awful." She sat there for a second, digesting this new information, and then said, "You don't think whoever did this is the one we're looking for, do you?"

"I don't know," I admitted. "Could be." I told her as much as I knew about Fluffy's murder. I even told her that poor Emmaline had decided to give up writing any more letters to the editor.

All the time I was talking, Cordelia just looked at me, her eyes growing huge. She put down her carrot uneaten.

When I was finished, Cordelia didn't say a word. She just sat there, thinking. Looking at her plate. At the other people in the dining room. At everybody but me.

The silence dragged on and on, until finally I couldn't stand it any more. I looked out the window and said, "It sure is a pretty night."

Talk about smooth.

I must've looked out the window for several minutes. Finally, having thoroughly absorbed the view, and also having grown tired of waiting for Cordelia to say something, I said, "By the way, you might have Eunice give me a phone call—the next time Joe Eddy isn't around."

Evidently, I was not anywhere near as smooth as I hoped. A flicker of alarm appeared in Cordelia's eyes. "Why do you want to talk to Eunice? You don't think *Joe Eddy* had anything to do with all this?"

"Of course not," I lied. "No, I just got the feeling Eunice might've been holding something back when I talked to her. That she couldn't really speak her mind in front of Joe Eddy."

Like, for example, Eunice couldn't tell me that her husband was a cold-blooded killer of people and animals. I could be wrong, of course, but now that I knew for certain that Joe Eddy had had access to the necessary information about Emmaline and her cats to put a hit on Fluffy, Joe Eddy looked like a prime suspect to me. It would be real interesting to find out where Joe Eddy was last night.

Cordelia looked somewhat placated. "Well, I'm going to be having dinner with them tomorrow night," she said. "I'll try to get Eunice alone and give her your message." She paused, and gave me another one of her mesmerizing blue-eyed glances. "I shouldn't say this, but sometimes I—I wish Eunice would go ahead and leave Joe Eddy. He's such a bully."

Well, we agreed on something. I wondered if Cordelia had any idea that Joe Eddy could be—how was it that Melba had put it?—"smacking" poor Eunice around. Looking at Cordelia's clear blue eyes, I decided she didn't have a clue. Which was odd. You'd think Eunice's sister would suspect a thing like that. Of course, who knew? Maybe Melba was wrong. Maybe it was just a rumor. Nothing more. It was easy, looking at Joe Eddy, to understand how a rumor like that could get started.

Mama Gentry brought our supper right about then, and for a while neither of us said anything. I hadn't realized how hungry I was until I smelled that fried chicken. It made your mouth water.

Cordelia had finished one piece and was wiping her hands on her napkin when she leaned across the table. "Grammy's fried chicken was every bit as good as this," she said.

I nodded at her. I would've said something, but my mouth was full.

Cordelia turned to look out the window, her eyes wistful now. "I sure wish you could've known Grammy, Haskell. You'd know then how special she was," she said. "She was a lot more than just a grandmother to Eunice and me."

My mouth was still too full for me to say anything, so I just nodded again. I started chewing faster, in case I needed to speak.

"After our mom and dad were killed in a car accident," Cordelia went on, "Grammy took me and Eunice in and finished raising us. She and Grampap were our whole family."

Poor kid. She looked almost forlorn suddenly. I'd swallowed by then, thank goodness, so I managed to say, "Really?" It was the best I could do on short notice.

Cordelia nodded. "Really," she said.

This time I did better. "How old were you two when you lost your parents?"

"Four. And Eunice was six."

Eunice had told me the same thing when I'd talked to her and Joe Eddy, but this time it really hit me. I looked at Cordelia and I didn't even blink. But I was thinking, do you mean to tell me that Eunice is only *two* years older than you? That poor dried-up woman looked at least ten years older than Cordelia.

Lord. Either Cordelia had found the Fountain of Youth, or else poor Eunice had discovered the less sought-after Well of Aging. I had a feeling Joe Eddy might've helped poor Eunice discover this particular well. Hell, he probably dug it for her.

Cordelia took a bite of green beans before she went on. "Grammy was so wonderful—back then she was hurting, too, losing her only son and his wife so sudden and all. But Grammy still had time for us— she used to kiss and hug us all the time." Cordelia's eyes were real misty now. "And she taught us a lot. Grammy taught us to walk around with our heads held high."

Grammy must've been quite a woman to inspire such devotion. I sat there, listening to Cordelia, and wondered which of the images of Grammy that I'd been given was the right one. Loving wife, devoted grandmother, or crazy lady and outrageous flirt? Could Grammy have been all of these things? It didn't seem possible.

"Grammy sounds like a remarkable woman, all right," I said. This time I was telling the truth. Grammy had to be a magician if she could be so many different things to so many different people. I picked up another piece of chicken. "Tell me, did Grammy ever mention in those letters of hers anybody who particularly disliked her pets?"

Cordelia's fork paused in midair. "You know, I've tried to think if she ever mentioned anybody. But, the only person who ever complained about her pets—as I recall—was Grammy."

I nodded. "Delbert Sims told me that they got on Grammy's nerves sometimes."

Cordelia shook her head. "The bird didn't bother her—Grammy adored Sweety-bird. No, it was just

Percival that she'd get mad at.'' Cordelia grinned here, and added, "Of course, you know why." Her look implied that a chimpanzee could figure this one out.

My face must've looked as blank as my mind. I wondered, was it okay for a detective to admit he hadn't figured something out yet? Or did it make clients think they were throwing away their money? I decided to risk it. "No, why?" I said.

Cordelia did look a tad disappointed. "That cat kept stalking poor Sweety-bird."

Oh. Well. A cat actually chasing a bird. Now who would ever think of such a thing? I took another bite of my chicken.

"When I was there at Christmas," Cordelia went on, "Grammy had to chase the cat outdoors quite a few times. And then, of course, Percival kept attacking your feet."

"Your feet?" I hoped this wasn't another one of those things I should've known. Cordelia might start demanding a refund.

Cordelia nodded. "That cat was stalking everything. It would jump at your feet every time you went into the same room it was in. Percival scratched holes into two pairs of my hose the week I was there."

I looked up from my chicken. "Had Percival ever acted like this before?"

Cordelia shook her head. "As far as I know, he hadn't. Of course, I didn't pay too much attention to Grammy's pets. She took care of them, you know, and usually, the cat and bird stayed pretty much out of the way. That Christmas was the first time I ever remember Percival acting so wild."

"I wonder why," I said.

Cordelia shrugged her pretty shoulders. "Maybe he

was just getting old and senile. He sure acted grouchy, though, you'd think—" Her voice abruptly quit, like a faucet that had been shut off. Then, her eyes got even larger as she looked at me. She didn't finish her sentence. Instead, Cordelia blinked a couple of times and said, "Do they serve dessert here?"

She was reaching for her plate, starting to lift it, when I put my hand out to stop her. "Pecan pie and ice cream, or banana cream pudding." That's what my mouth said. My mind, however, was thinking, *Now what suddenly occurred to Cordelia that she doesn't want to tell me?*

Because something *had* occurred to her. It was written all over her pretty face. It may not occur to me that cats chase birds, but I can read faces. Cordelia's face was talking loud and clear.

The rest of the evening I kept thinking about it off and on. What does Cordelia know about that cat of Grammy's that she clearly doesn't want to tell me?

The whole problem gave me something to think about on the way home. Other than, of course, whether I should try to kiss Cordelia after I walked her to the door.

Planting one on a client didn't seem like a terribly professional thing to do. And yet, when I was around Cordelia, I didn't feel real professional.

Cordelia herself, however, finally made up my mind for me. She turned to me, just as we were walking up the steps to Robey's Boarding House and said, "Thanks, Haskell. I really do appreciate everything you're doing."

My mind went completely blank for a second. Finally, I managed to get out, "No problem."

And she kissed me. Right on the mouth, her body warm against mine.

What a woman.

Right away, however, Cordelia pulled away. "So—what's your next move?" she asked.

Well, I think I'll just kiss you a couple of hundred more times and then try to get you in bed. That's what I thought. I had already opened my mouth to give her the condensed version of that, when—thank goodness— it occurred to me that Cordelia was talking about the *case.*

It was like being hit with a splash of cold water. I blinked a couple of times, swallowed once, and said, "I reckon I'll be talking to Ray Don Peters' neighbors tomorrow."

Cordelia looked confused. "I thought you said Ray Don didn't have anything to do with all this."

"No, what I said was that Ray Don wasn't a suspect. I never said Ray Don wasn't involved." In fact, I had no idea whether he was involved or not. "I just think it's odd how often his name keeps coming up," I said. "Real odd."

"You'll let me know what you find out, won't you? Right away?" Cordelia asked.

"Sure," I said. "No problem."

For my reward, Cordelia gave me a dazzling smile as she swept into the boarding house.

CHAPTER TEN

Ray Don Peters was still listed in the Pigeon Fork Telephone Directory. This, of course, was no surprise. It would've been a surprise had he *not* been there.

The people who do the phone book here in Pigeon Fork apparently don't update it until they're certain it really needs it. I found that out the first week I was back, and I tried to use the thing. A lot of the numbers had been disconnected.

Elmo told me then that it takes the phone book people at least two years before they fully realize that you're either dead or you've moved out of town. I guess they want to make sure you're good and gone before they go to all the trouble of erasing your name.

This is, of course, assuming that the phone book people ever do actually get around to erasing your name. I have my doubts. Personally, I wouldn't be at all surprised to see people listed in the Pigeon Fork Directory who'd been killed in the Civil War.

I recognized the address next to Ray Don's name.

It was only about three miles from my office, on one of several quiet tree-lined side streets that intersect Main Street. It wouldn't take any time at all to get over there.

Before I left, though, I thought I'd better give Melba a call, just to see if perhaps hell had frozen overnight and she actually had some messages for me. Also, I figured, after the terrific job she'd no doubt done yesterday answering my phone while I was gone, I just might want to make sure that today Melba was well aware that I was going to be away from my office for a spell.

As quick as I could say, "Melba, this is Haskell," I could feel the phone lines frosting up.

"Oh." Melba's voice was crisp. "It's you."

Great. So Melba *was* mad at me, after all, for not letting her do any questioning. I took a deep breath. Melba doesn't realize it, but I've had a lot of practice dealing with an irate woman. I immediately went into Defense Stance Number One—Pretend You Don't Notice She's Upset. This one worked pretty good with Claudzilla, being as how she didn't think I was any too bright, anyway. "Well, howdy, how're you doing," I said, real cheery. "I just wanted to check in with you and see if there were any messages."

"Nope."

I swallowed. "Well, I'm going to be out of my office for a while, so I thought I'd just let you know." My voice couldn't get any cheerier. I sounded like a Welcome Wagon lady.

Melba grunted.

"And I wanted to tell you that I sure appreciate your help, Melba," I said. "I really do." Lord.

Melba grunted again, and roused herself to speak. "I reckon I'd be a lot more inclined to answer your phone, Haskell, if I felt like I was more a *part* of things."

I swallowed again. "Now, Melba, I've always considered you a part of things, you know that." At that moment, she probably didn't want to know the exact part I considered her. "You're a real help to me, Melba. Doing what you do best. Keeping my office running smoothly." I wondered if any second my nose was going to start to grow.

Melba was apparently unimpressed with my sincerity. She grunted a third time and hung up on me.

I drove on over to Ray Don's house, fervently hoping that no one happened to call me anytime soon.

Ray Don's place turned out to be a small, white frame house with red shutters and a black shingled roof. It looked exactly like the small, white frame house next door, the one with blue shutters and a black shingled roof.

Both had a neat square of lawn in front, and a screened porch on the side. The only thing that distinguished the two houses—besides the bold individuality expressed by the color of their shutters—was the large flower garden in the side yard of the house that had been Ray Don's. The garden took up the entire side yard, and it looked as if it had recently exploded with orange, red, and yellow mums. At the back of the garden stood a lot of tall flowers that looked just like big orange lilies.

The flower garden looked real nice until I got out of my truck and walked toward the house next door. Then I could clearly see that the lilies and particularly the mums were sharing garden space with a lot of weeds. In a couple of places, there didn't seem to be anything but weeds.

A small, white-haired woman in a pink dress was

sitting out in a lawn chair on the screen porch of the blue-shuttered house. She had been reading when I pulled up. As I got out of my truck, she lifted her hand to shade her face. So that she could stare at me without the sun's glare on her glasses.

I recognized her right away. It was Mrs. Old Foot. Actually, her name was Offutt, but my brother Elmo and all the other kids in his seventh-grade English class called her Old Foot. Not to her face, of course.

Back then, that name had seemed like a real hoot. Now, it just seems silly. Of course, a lot of things that sounded real funny to you when you were a kid don't exactly stand the test of time.

Speaking of which, it had to be almost twenty-five years ago that Mrs. Offutt had Elmo in her class, and she was no spring chicken then. As I recall, Elmo used to speculate that one day they'd come back from lunch and find her dead behind her desk. "Croaked," I believe, was the term he'd used.

Apparently, Elmo had badly miscalculated.

When I was within hearing distance, I started to introduce myself. I didn't expect Mrs. Offutt to remember me, being as how I was never in any of her classes. Before I could open my mouth, though, the old woman said, "Why, aren't you Elmo Blevins's brother? The spy?"

This is another thing you get used to around these parts. People know you—sort of. They've talked to somebody who knows somebody who knows somebody else who possibly has actually met you. Or maybe not. Maybe they've just heard of you. Whatever Mrs. Offutt had heard, it was obviously wrong.

I smiled at her, anyway. "I'm Elmo's brother, all right," I said, "but I'm a detective. Not a spy."

Eighty-five if she was a day, Mrs. Offutt took her

hand away from her eyes and gave me an elaborate wink. "Whatever you say," she said, her hazel eyes twinkling behind her thin wire frames. "I know you guys are always working undercover."

This little old lady had been watching too much TV.

I decided, though, that it wasn't worth getting into. I just went right on. "I'm Haskell Blevins, and I need to ask you a few questions."

Mrs. Offutt looked literally tickled pink. Her cheeks were suddenly rosy with excitement. "Really?" she said. She looked cautiously around us, and then whispered, "Is it one of my neighbors?"

I had lost her. "Who?"

"The man you're spying on." Mrs. Offutt looked around us again. "Is he a traitor—or maybe one of those foreign agents? I've heard tell they're all around us now—living just like normal folk in small towns all across these United States!" She squinted down the street as if she half expected to see a Russian tank coming over the hill.

I hated to disappoint her. "No, ma'am, matter of fact, I'm not snooping on anybody," I said.

Her face fell.

"Of course," I added, "if I were, I wouldn't be able to tell you."

Her small face brightened. "Why, that's right," she said eagerly. "It's—um, classy-fied information, isn't it?"

I looked straight at her and nodded solemnly. Like maybe this was some big conspiracy we were talking about. The things I do to keep people happy.

And Mrs. Offutt was happy, all right. She looked as if any minute she might clap her bony little hands together in sheer delight. I had made her day.

She closed the book on her lap—*The Spy Who Came in from the Cold*—with a loud thunk, and turned her full attention to me. You could almost hear what she was thinking. Why read a piece of fiction when you can experience it in person?

In less than five minutes, I knew that her full name was Beatrice Offutt, that she had retired from teaching about twenty years ago, and that she spent a lot of her time these days reading John Le Carré novels. I also learned that she'd been widowed in her forties, that she had two children and six grandchildren and one great-grandchild—and that, oh yes, incidentally, she'd lived next door to Ray Don Peters for almost eight years. Ray Don had bought the house next door when its former occupants had gotten themselves divorced.

"My, yes, Ray Don was a wonderful neighbor," Mrs. Offutt said. I'd sat myself down in the lawn chair next to her by then, and I could tell she was enjoying herself. All the time she was talking, she fiddled with the lace at her collar excitedly.

It was a warm day, but Mrs. Offutt's dress had a high collar and long sleeves. The skirt reached all the way to her ankles. As I recalled, she'd worn similar outfits back when she was teaching. Either she was real cold-natured, or Mrs. Offutt had made being prim a science. "And Ray Don kept his yard looking so nice," she was going on. "Not like the neighbors I got now."

She looked over at the house next door disdainfully, and started whispering again. "That young couple who moved in next door—they've just let Ray Don's garden go all to pot. He would *die* if he knew!" It seemed to occur to her then that Ray Don had already done his dying, because she stopped for a second. "Well," she said, waving a thin hand airily, "you know what I mean."

I did. "I guess it was pretty awful having somebody die like that right next door and all."

Mrs. Offutt nodded gleefully. "Oh, yes, it was terrible!" Her eyes danced. "I found him, you know."

"You discovered the body?"

Mrs. Offutt shrugged. "Well, sort of. I went over there to give Ray Don some late squash out of my garden. Him being a bachelor and all, I kind of looked after him. Anyway, he wouldn't answer the door, so after a while I called the police."

"Oh?" I said. Had I missed something? Hadn't she said she found the body?

Mrs. Offutt hurried on eagerly, "And, after the police got here, I discovered *them* discovering the body!"

"No kidding," I said. I tried to look impressed.

Mrs. Offutt leaned toward me. "Was Ray Don a spy, too?" She was whispering once again.

I shook my head and whispered back, "We don't think so."

Once again, I watched Mrs. Offutt's face fall. She looked like a little wrinkled kid who'd been disappointed Christmas morning. "Of course"—here I looked around us elaborately—"you do realize, I wouldn't be able to tell you even if he were."

Mrs. Offutt's face brightened just like Christmas lights being turned on. "Oh, this is awful!" she said delightedly.

I nodded. It really was.

"Tell me, Mrs. Offutt," I said, "did Ray Don ever mention a Mrs. Turley to you?"

Mrs. Offutt reached out a gnarled hand and touched my shoulder. "Now, let's have none of that," she said, smiling. "It's Beatrice to you." Behind her glasses, thin gray eyelashes batted coquettishly at me.

I smiled back at her. Beatrice Offutt really was a charmer. But I couldn't imagine actually calling a *teacher* by her first name. Not even now, when we were both adults. Just thinking about it in front of her made me feel a little uneasy—as if, any second now, Mrs. Offutt might whip out a ruler and rap my knuckles with it.

"I was asking about whether Ray Don ever mentioned a Mrs. Turley?" I reminded her.

Mrs. Offutt's hazel eyes stopped twinkling at me. "Grammy? Oh, of course Ray Don mentioned her. She was over there all the time." She cocked her head at me. "Alone. Just the two of them. And her a married woman."

I was working on trying to look shocked when Mrs. Offutt hurried on, "Grammy told me they were just discussing gardening, but, well, I told *her* that it didn't look good. That folks would gossip. And that she should be careful about her reputation."

From what I'd heard of Grammy, I bet that went over like a lead balloon.

Sure enough, Mrs. Offutt pointed a bony finger at me. "But you know what Grammy did? She just laughed at me. Can you imagine? She *laughed!*" Even now, there was still a trace of shock in Mrs. Offutt's hazel eyes.

I suspected it didn't take a whole lot to shock Mrs. Offutt. Perhaps wearing colors that clashed would do it.

"Then you knew Grammy personally?"

Mrs. Offutt gave me another sweet smile. "Of course I did. Everybody knew Grammy."

146

She leaned toward me again, and I knew before she opened her mouth, she'd be whispering again. "I know poor Grammy's dead now and all—but, Lordy, she was just shameless!"

"Really?" I said.

Mrs. Offutt nodded her snowy head. "Really! You should've seen her at Ray Don's funeral! It was just awful the way she hung all over Delbert Sims, crying and carrying on. With her own husband standing right there!"

Well, now, this didn't seem too bad. Maybe Grammy had just been upset, and Delbert's shoulder had been the nearest one to cry on. The only problem with it that I could see was the strong possibility of Delbert's shoulder not being any too reliable. If I'd been Grammy, I would've been afraid that if I leaned on Delbert's shoulder, I might end up flat on my face on the floor of the church.

Mrs. Offutt had raised her snowy eyebrows and was looking at me over the top of her wireframes. As if to say, *See? Wasn't Grammy a floozy?* I clucked my tongue, and tried to look more than shocked. I tried to look appalled.

Mrs. Offutt looked appalled enough for the both of us. "Grammy was a—a—*brazen hussy*." She whispered those last two words. If she was going to keep doing this, I was going to have to move closer.

"No kidding," I said. I knew I'd said it before, but I'd already used "Really?" I shook my head, disbelievingly.

Mrs. Offutt was shaking her head, too. "Grammy always had to be the center of attention. Always."

This didn't seem too terrible, either. So Grammy liked a little attention. Big deal.

It was apparently a big deal to Mrs. Offutt. She was

still shaking her head, disapproval in every shake. A couple of hair pins fell onto the top of her book. "I mean to tell you, Grammy would do anything for attention."

"She would?" That might explain Grammy's orangey-red hair.

Mrs. Offutt leaned close again. This time, though, she apparently forgot to whisper. "You know what Grammy told me right after Ray Don's funeral?" Mrs. Offutt said, putting her hair pins back in. "I mean, *right* after the funeral?"

I was game. "No, what?"

"Grammy said she knew something she couldn't tell anybody on account of it could land somebody in jail."

I was suddenly alert. "Grammy told you this? And did you tell the sheriff?"

Mrs. Offutt smiled and shook her head again. "No! Of course not," she said. "It was just Grammy's way of trying to grab the spotlight." Mrs. Offutt pursed her lips into a small, thin line, her eyes narrowing. "Can you believe it? I reckon Grammy would've had us all believe that Ray Don had been murdered—and that she alone knew who'd done it!"

For a minute, I couldn't speak. This was something. I cleared my throat. "Did Grammy actually say she knew somebody had killed Ray Don? That it wasn't an accident?"

Mrs. Offutt frowned, thinking back. "Well, no, not in so many words. But what else could it be about?"

Actually, it could've been about anything. Maybe Grammy had stumbled onto something that she shouldn't have. Maybe she'd been killed because she was a danger to somebody.

On the other hand, let's not forget that this *was*

Grammy we were talking about—the woman who five months later wouldn't even remember that Ray Don was dead. It didn't really seem necessary to shut Grammy up. She seemed to do that very nicely all by herself.

Mrs. Offutt wasn't finished, though. "Can you believe it? Grammy told us that knowing full well that Ray Don's death was nothing more than an accident. That's how bad she needed attention. She would make things up if she had to!"

"Did you ever think for a minute that Ray Don's death wasn't an accident?"

"No!" Mrs. Offutt looked at me as if I'd suddenly taken leave of my senses. Then, as a thought suddenly occurred to her, her expression changed. "—unless, of course, Ray Don was working undercover," she said. She cocked her snowy head at me hopefully.

I shook my head. "He wasn't."

Mrs. Offutt didn't buy it. "I knew you'd say that," she said. "I knew you wouldn't tell me even if he was, now, would you?"

I decided to change the subject. "Did you happen to know Myrldean Bleemel, too?"

Mrs. Offutt's eyes got very wide behind those glasses of hers. "Was she a spy, too?"

I was getting tired of this. "Nope. She wasn't." At the doubtful look on Mrs. Offutt's face, I added, "Really. She wasn't."

Mrs. Offutt looked disappointed.

"I can't help it," I said. "She wasn't a spy. Never. Ever."

Mrs. Offutt looked as if she might cry.

I decided to ignore her. "Is Myrldean's family still in town?" I was thinking maybe I should go see them next. Hopefully, they'd never heard of me. And, none of them had ever read a spy novel.

Mrs. Offutt, however, was shaking her head. "All Myrldean had left was her husband, Ned, and he moved out of town over a year ago. After he got married again."

She said this last sentence the same way you might say "After he got anthrax."

"Do you know where he moved to?"

Mrs. Offutt ignored the question, intent on telling me the entire terrible story of how Ned had betrayed the dearly departed Myrldean. "Less than a year after poor Myrldean passed away," Mrs. Offutt said, "Ned Bleemel up and married a woman ten years younger than him. *Ten years.*" On those last two words, Mrs. Offutt went back to whispering again. As if it were a scandal too awful to speak out loud. "A man his age, doing a thing like that!" she added.

"My, my," I said. "How old exactly is Ned Bleemel?"

Mrs. Offutt fluffed her white hair. "Oh, let me see. In his late seventies, I guess. Poor Myrldean was seventy-two when she died. And she wasn't even cold in her grave when Ned took himself another bride!" Mrs. Offutt seemed intent on making sure that I grasped the enormity of Ned's transgression.

Let me see now. Ned Bleemel was in his seventies, and he married someone in her sixties. What a wild man.

I leaned toward Mrs. Offutt, and lowered my voice. "You know, I heard that Myrldean and Grammy used to fight quite a bit."

Mrs. Offutt looked surprised. "Oh, no, that isn't so. They were real good friends. Right up until the end." She fiddled with her lace collar again. "Toward the end maybe they had a couple of little tiffs, like old friends do." Mrs. Offutt looked straight at me, the lens in her glasses making her eyes look huge. "You might as well know that Myrldean was a mite crochety those last months. You know how you get."

As a matter of fact, I didn't. But I nodded anyway.

"I wasn't real surprised when Myrldean died," Mrs. Offutt went on. "She'd fallen down her front steps before, you know. Broke her hip the first time. The last time I guess she just hit her head too hard."

"A shame," I said.

Mrs. Offutt nodded sadly. "By the way," she said, "are you married?"

Oh dear. In Pigeon Fork these are dangerous words. I don't know what it is with the women around here. It's as if they have some kind of conspiracy among themselves—to make sure no single man goes unchallenged.

If I had seen this coming, I could've tried to change the subject. As it was, there didn't seem to be anything to do but tell Mrs. Offutt the truth. For one thing, she'd find out from whoever it was that had told her I was a spy that I was single. "I'm recently divorced," I said between gritted teeth.

The hazel eyes behind Mrs. Offutt's frames seemed to grow even larger. "Why, I do declare," she said, happily. "Let me show you a portrait of my granddaughter. She's going to be visiting me soon, and I think you two might really hit it off."

She bustled off indoors, her long pink skirt rustling away. While she was inside, I actually considered leaving, but I hadn't finished questioning her yet. Besides, Mrs. Offutt was an attractive woman for her age, how bad could her granddaughter be?

When I saw that portrait, I knew. If there was such

151

a thing as a bad gene pool, poor Mrs. Offutt's grand-daughter had swum in it. The only thing this woman shared with Mrs. Offutt was the glasses. She had a long jaw, a long nose, and long, lank hair. Through which her ears poked. I had to pretend my jaw was wired shut to keep it from dropping open.

"Isn't she intelligent-looking?" Mrs. Offutt asked.

I smiled at her uncertainly. I hoped this woman was intelligent. Otherwise, it was a complete loss.

"I'll just have to give you a call when she gets in town," Mrs. Offutt said.

"Hmm," I said. I've been introduced to cousins, daughters, nieces, granddaughters, grandnieces, you name it. Until I moved here, I wouldn't have believed there could be so many unattached female relatives in the world.

Unfortunately, when I met them, I realized real quick how come it was that these particular women remained unattached. The ones that were pretty had tongues that could cut through barbed wire, and the ones that were ugly weren't just ugly—they were beyond ugly. Reaching a whole new dimension of ugly.

And Mrs. Offutt's granddaughter? She was boldly going where ugly had never been before.

"I just know you two are going to be a real match," Mrs. Offutt was saying.

Sure we were. Like Beauty and the Beast. Only *I* would play the part of Beauty. Which was a scary thought. I hurriedly changed the subject. "Did Myrldean ever say anything to you those last weeks that might have struck you as odd?"

"Why, what do you mean?" Mrs. Offutt said. At least, she'd put her granddaughter's portrait away.

"Like, did she say she was fighting with anybody—

or that she'd seen any strangers around her house? Anything like that?"

Mrs. Offutt shook her head doubtfully. "It's been two years, you know. The only thing I can remember her complaining about was Delbert Sims."

"Delbert?" I couldn't keep the surprise out of my voice.

Mrs. Offutt folded her small arms across her chest, and nodded. "Myrldean said Delbert tried to kill her dog."

I was more astounded at this than I was at the portrait of her granddaughter. Which was saying a lot.

"He tried to kill her dog?"

"Myrldean had one of those little Cockapoo dogs— you know the kind, it looks like a big white mouse with a permanent?"

I nodded.

"Well, Myrldean carried it around with her everywhere. Even to the grocery. She rode it around in her basket, and one day it got loose in the Crayton County Supermarket. Myrldean told me that Delbert found her dog before she did." Mrs. Offutt stopped and just looked at me, as if that said it all.

"And?" I said.

"And Delbert was about to give Myrldean's dog a kick into the middle of next week when Myrldean rushed up, all upset, and snatched it right out from under his foot." Mrs. Offutt waved her bony hands in the air. "It was so exciting! The whole town was talking about it. You know, Delbert Sims isn't—isn't very nice."

Apparently, this was the worst thing she could bring herself to say about him. "He's a scamp," I said.

Mrs. Offutt agreed. "He certainly is."

Delbert was already at the top of the sheriff's list of possible suspects, and he had just climbed to the top of mine. I was beginning to think maybe I needed to watch this scamp a little more closely. That maybe if I hung around his house for a while, I might see something that the scamp might not want me to see. It was a thought.

Another thought was how to get away from Mrs. Offutt without having to promise I'd meet her granddaughter.

This thought proved impossible. Mrs. Offutt wouldn't let me leave. She stood there, blocking my way, jabbering about her granddaughter, until I realized it was hopeless. Short of running right over a little, white-haired old lady, there was nothing else I could do.

I actually found myself saying, "Sure, when your granddaughter gets in town, call me. I'll be looking forward to it."

Mrs. Offutt had missed her calling; she ought to be overseas right this minute, negotiating the release of hostages.

Once Mrs. Offutt had released *me,* I decided to drive on home. If I was going to do surveillance on Delbert, I had better feed Rip and carry him up- and downstairs. I wasn't sure how long I'd be watching old Delbert, so I intended to fill Rip's bowls to overflowing.

Rip was doing his usual "bark at the guy who lives here" routine when I got out of my truck. He seemed in particularly good form today, standing up there at the top of the steps, barking to beat the band without stopping once to take a breath.

I was just starting my climb up the stairs, saying,

154

"Good boy, Rip, good boy. You're scaring me to death," when I felt something soft and yielding under my shoe.

For a second I thought maybe Rip had been cured. If what I had stepped in, however, was what I thought it was, Rip's fear of stairs was about to be replaced by a brand-new fear. Fear of being hit about the head and shoulders with a rolled-up newspaper.

I lifted my shoe very gingerly. At the top of the stairs, Rip had stopped barking and was just looking at me, his head cocked to one side.

What I'd stepped in was a small mound of hamburger. It had been placed on the bottom step on a piece of lined notepaper. Part of the paper was sticking out from under the ground beef.

On this part of the paper someone had written in a by-now familiar hand:

YOUR NEXT.

CHAPTER

ELEVEN

Even over the phone, it was real clear that Vergil was irritated again. He didn't even have a pet, for God's sake, and he was mad because someone had tried to kill mine.

I had had it. I felt like telling him, okay, Vergil, get yourself a cat or a dog, and I'll be glad to come on by and poison it for you.

"I can't believe this," Vergil grumbled. "I'm working on this case, too, you know—and nobody's done nothing to me."

"What can I say, Vergil?" I think I sounded downright sympathetic, considering how I really felt.

"I just don't get it," Vergil said. "I just talked to Delbert Sims yesterday, too. It's not like I'm doing nothing on this case."

"Did Delbert have anything interesting to say?" I wasn't just trying to change the subject. I really did want to know. Although if by any chance the subject did happen to change, it wouldn't be the worst thing in the world.

Vergil didn't answer me right away. It makes you real uneasy to be suddenly talking to dead silence.

"Vergil?" I said.

"Delbert didn't say much," Vergil said, his voice mournful as usual. Something about the way Vergil said it, though, made me wonder if he was being totally honest. Maybe Vergil had finally decided that I really was poaching on too much of his territory. Maybe he wasn't going to be sharing any more free information with me.

"Did Delbert say anything at all?" I asked.

"Not really." It was hard for me to believe that Vergil had talked to Delbert yesterday, face to face, and Delbert hadn't said one word. How does a conversation like that go? It was definitely looking like Vergil had clammed up on me. Great. Just great. This sure wasn't going to make things any easier.

"I reckon you expect me to come all the way out there and get the evidence," Vergil was saying. "Up that steep driveway of yours." He sounded put-upon.

"I reckon," I said. I live seven miles from where Vergil was standing that very minute. A ten minute drive if you crawled. Vergil made it sound as if I lived a hundred miles away and that the entire drive was uphill.

"I don't know why you can't just bring the evidence on in," Vergil said. "We're sure not going to find anything, anyway, except that the meat's been poisoned. I just got back the reports on your note and Emmaline Johnston's window, and that's all the state lab came up with. They found out that the meat was full of rat poison."

If I had been Rip, my ears would've pricked up. "You mean to tell me there weren't any fingerprints on the note or the window?"

Vergil sounded real annoyed this time. Like maybe he thought I wasn't paying attention or something. "I said there wasn't nothing, didn't I? Nothing on your note. Whoever wrote it must've been smart enough to wear gloves."

I had to admit, the culprit was beginning to sound less and less like Joe Eddy.

"And nothing on the window at Emmaline Johnston's," Vergil went on. "It had been wiped clean."

"Hmm," I said.

"Hmm yourself," Vergil said. He was clearly in a snit.

"Well, Vergil, don't you think you ought to mosey on out here and take a look at the crime scene?" I made my voice sound a lot more patient than I felt.

"Ain't been no crime. Your dog ain't even been hurt." Was I imagining it, or did Vergil sound a little disappointed that it had turned out this way?

I was getting irritated. "Look, Vergil, don't you think you'd better come on out here and at least go through the motions, in case somebody slipped up? I mean, it would look real bad if I had to call up one of my old friends from Louisville." This was a total bluff. I couldn't think of a single person who would drive all the way to Pigeon Fork on account of my dog being *almost* poisoned.

It worked, though. On the other end of the line, I could hear Vergil sigh. I could also hear him say a couple of curse words under his breath. This was one of only two times that I have ever wished my phone didn't work so well.

The other was about two months ago when Claudzilla called me all the way from Louisville to tell me everything she hated about me. She said, among other things, that I was a real negative person who never had a good thing to say about anybody. I was shocked. After all the terribly nice things I've said about *her*.

Claudzilla's psychiatrist had suggested that telling me all the reasons she hated my guts would be a "cleansing" experience for her. Her psychiatrist had apparently given no thought at all to what kind of experience it would be for me.

"Oh, all right," Vergil said shortly, "I'll be there in a while." It seemed to me that he hung up the phone with a little more force than absolutely necessary.

I hung up, too—if a bit later than Vergil—and I went over to pet Rip again. He was lying on the kitchen floor blocking the doorway, so that if you wanted to leave the room, you had to step over him. For some reason, this is always the spot Rip picks to lie down in. Usually, this is real irritating, but today I thought it was kind of cute.

I guess, up until today, I had never fully realized how much I liked my mentally ill dog. "Good boy," I said for no reason, really. "Good boy, Rip." This is something that Rip apparently can't hear enough, because he always acts as if he were hearing it for the first time. He got up, and started jumping and dancing around, and trying to lick me on the mouth.

I backed away, protecting my lips, and opened the fridge. While I was talking to Vergil, I'd decided to give Rip one of the rib eyes I'd been saving to barbecue. Rip deserved a reward for making it through this day, still breathing.

There was no doubt whatsoever that Vergil would find that the hamburger lying out on my bottom step was as full of rat poison as Emmaline's. In fact, I could almost see in my mind how the whole scene had gone.

Whoever had intended to poison Rip had driven up,

watched Rip doing his snarling psycho-dog routine at the top of the steps, and decided not to venture any closer than the bottom step. In fact, from the way the hamburger looked, sort of crumbled around the edges, it might've been dropped out of a car window.

Whoever had done this did not know me very well, or he would've known about Rip's stairs phobia. I complain about it often enough. I would never have guessed in a million years that I'd be glad Rip was afraid to go downstairs. If Rip hadn't been such a nut, though, he would most certainly be winning a Fluffy look-alike contest this very minute. Instead of sitting there right in front of me, wagging his silly tail.

I decided to warm up Rip's rib eye in the microwave. To give him a real special treat. While I was doing that, I couldn't help but smile. More than once I'd tried to coax Rip down the stairs with big hunks of sirloin steak. Did the would-be dog killer think Rip would really come down for *hamburger?*

"You're a classy dog, Rip," I told him, putting the rib eye in front of him. "You've got taste."

Rip didn't touch it for a second. Instead, he just sat there, looking at me, his head cocked to one side, the way he does. As if to say, *Is this some kind of trick?* "Go ahead, boy," I said.

I didn't have to say it twice.

Rip had just started chewing on his steak, a surprised and delighted look on his face, when the phone rang. I recognized Eunice's hesitant voice. "Mr. Blevins? Cordelia's here and she said you—you wanted to talk to me?"

"That's right," I said. I wondered if Rip would like a little steak sauce. The phone cord was long enough for me to reach the fridge. I decided to get it for him. "I wondered if there wasn't something that you might've remembered since I talked to you last."

I took off the cap, and poured the thick dark sauce all over Rip's steak. He looked at me. Either gratitude was in his eyes, or disbelief. I decided it was gratitude.

"Oh, Mr. Blevins, I—I really can't think of a thing. I told you everything I know," Eunice said. Her voice shook a little. "Cordelia's right here—do you want to talk to her?" Eunice seemed awful anxious to get off the phone considering she was the one who called me. I wondered what was going on.

"I'd like to talk to Cordelia in a minute, yes," I said, "but there was one thing I wanted to ask you." I was scrambling in my mind for what it was that had bothered me. What was it, for God's sake? Evidently, Rip's near-miss had shook me up more than I thought.

"Yes?" Eunice sounded scared. And impatient.

I suddenly remembered. "You know the new seed catalogue that you were going to loan Grammy?"

There was total silence on the other end. I couldn't even hear Eunice breathing. Finally, she said, her voice shaking even more, "What seed catalogue? I never said nothing about—"

"Delbert Sims mentioned it to me. He said that you were going to loan your new catalogue to Grammy on account of her not getting hers in the mail yet."

Silence again. What was she doing? Fainting in between sentences? "Oh, yes," Eunice eventually said. She still sounded doubtful.

"Well, when I went over to talk to Grampap," I said, "all I saw over there was last year's catalogue."

This time Eunice answered real quick. "Oh, that's because Grammy forgot to take mine home with her. She left it on my kitchen table. The catalogue is still over here." There was a pause, and then Eunice added, "Grammy forgot things a lot."

"Oh," I said, "I see. Well, that sure explains it, all right. Listen, can I talk to Cordelia—" I hadn't even finished when Cordelia came on the line.

"Haskell?" Her voice sounded worried.

"Well, things seem to be heating up some. Somebody just tried to kill my dog."

"Oh, no." Cordelia sounded alarmed, but her full attention seemed to be elsewhere. "Is your dog okay?"

"Rip's fine. The guy who tried to poison him missed. Listen, I wanted to let you know I'm going to be out of my office for a little while, so that if you need to reach me, leave a message with Melba."

It was fifty-fifty whether I'd actually get the message —particularly since Melba wasn't any too happy with me lately—but Melba was better than nothing.

Cordelia didn't answer right away. Now I was sure she was only half listening to me. Finally, she said, "Oh. Right. Okay. Um, Haskell, I've got to go right now. I'll talk to you later, okay?" She hung up.

Was I imagining it or was everybody involved in this case beginning to act strange? I wondered if something peculiar really was going on over there at Eunice's, or if it was just that Joe Eddy had walked in and Cordelia didn't want to be caught talking to me on the phone. Behind his back, so to speak.

It was over an hour before Vergil finally showed up in my driveway. While I was waiting, I got all my surveillance gear together, and I made a call to Melba.

My intention was to see if there were any messages— fat chance—and to smooth things over some more. I mean, there had to be some way I could convince Melba that she didn't really want to be doing any detective work. It shouldn't be hard. Lord knows, she didn't seem to want to be doing any other kind of work.

Unfortunately, I didn't get much of a chance to say anything. As soon as Melba recognized my voice, she said, "No messages," and hung up.

I stood there motionless for a second, listening to the dial tone. Because of the way the telephone districts are divided out here, or some such thing, it happens to be long distance for me to call Pigeon Fork from here—even though I have a Pigeon Fork address. I think this is one of the joys of living in the country that real estate folks sometimes forget to mention. Anyway, I figured that the enlightening conversation I'd just had with Melba cost me about a buck-fifty a word.

Tomorrow morning, first thing, I was going to have myself a serious talk with that woman. Enough was enough.

For the rest of the hour I was waiting for Vergil, I just sat around, played a little with Rip, and tried to keep the flies off the hamburger on my front step.

Rip started barking the second Vergil's car appeared in front of the house. The dog seemed absolutely delighted to have somebody besides me to bark at. He ran happily around the porch, alternating barks and growls. Snarling and baring his teeth. It was quite a performance.

This was evidently Rip's second performance of the day, having no doubt put on a display like this for his poisoner earlier. The experience of having two cars besides mine appear in the driveway in a single day was apparently too much for him. Rip was beside himself. In fact, it took me quite a while to chase Rip around the deck and get a grip on his collar so I could drag him, whining like a baby, inside. That goofy dog acted as if I were shutting off his favorite TV program.

Vergil was not amused. He sat out in his car the

163

whole time I was chasing Rip all over the deck, waiting and looking sadder than I'd ever seen Vergil look. Which was going some. Vergil was grumbling the second he set foot out of his car. "I don't mind telling you that I don't understand all this."

I didn't want to discuss it. "Thanks for getting over here so quick, Vergil," I said.

Vergil went right on, not even looking at me. He bent over and started putting the hamburger and the note into an evidence bag. "Nobody's done nothing to me. Nothing." He looked up in the middle of what he was doing to give me a mournful look. "Not a damn thing."

"You don't say," I said.

Vergil didn't say. He just raised his eyebrows at me, indicating without saying a word that it was all my fault. I was grabbing all the glory. All the tire-slashing, pet-poisoning glory. I wondered if maybe I could get Rip to bite him.

For all his grumbling, it took Vergil only five minutes to gather together all the evidence he apparently intended to take with him. I noticed that Vergil hadn't brought anybody with him to dust for fingerprints, but I didn't say anything. I figured that was probably pushing it.

I was, however, starting to feel real angry. Not just at Vergil, either. Some fool out there actually thought that he could get rid of me by killing a poor, defenseless animal. Watching Rip inside, jumping at the window, clawing at the curtains, barking and whining and carrying on, made me realize just how cruel this fool was. Anybody who would kill the mentally ill was slime.

I waited until Vergil left, still grumbling to himself, of course, before I put on my surveillance outfit. I waited because I didn't want Vergil asking me what I was doing in that getup. Vergil knows I'm not a hunter, so he would want to know for sure why on earth I was wearing the camouflage fatigues that a lot of hunters wear around here.

I would've hated to explain.

Here in Pigeon Fork I've had to come up with a whole new way of surveillance. Back in Louisville you could sit in an unmarked car across the street from a given location, and you could watch for whoever it was you were keeping an eye on. Out here, that doesn't work.

I tried it when I was working on the Feedsack Caper. I sat in my truck across the street from Toomey's Hardware Store, and I watched for suspicious goings-on. Within twenty minutes, I had three people come up to me and say, "Hi, Haskell, what are you doing here?"

I figured out right away that the sitting-in-the-unmarked-car kind of surveillance just doesn't fly around these parts. A couple of the people who came up to me during that twenty-minute span offered me a lift. They just assumed that my truck was broken down. Why else would I be sitting out there like that? I had a real tough time coming up with a convincing lie. I told one of them I was listening to my favorite song on the radio. He looked at me as if I were nuts.

I decided then that in Pigeon Fork you need a more basic kind of surveillance. A more down-to-earth, no-nonsense kind. The kind where you put on camouflage, and hide in the shrubbery. This kind of surveillance is not as dignified as sitting in an unmarked car, but it's a lot less humiliating than having the guy you're watching come up and ask you if you need a lift anywhere.

I carried Rip up- and downstairs one final time, put his dishes indoors, and locked him inside. Being as how I hardly ever left him alone indoors at night, Rip was hurt. Standing at the window, Rip gave me a look that reminded me of Vergil.

"Sorry, boy," I said, "but it's for your own good." Rip continued to look at me as if I'd just left him in a maximum-security prison, so I said, "I'll be back real soon." Rip's expression didn't change. He had no idea what I was saying, but he knew it wasn't good.

He didn't even bark at me when I got in the truck. He was that depressed. And that intent on making me feel guilty. Maybe Claudzilla had taught him better than I thought.

It took me about fifteen minutes to get to Delbert's house. I ended up driving about a mile past the turn-off to his house, right on by the Crayton County Supermarket, rounding the bend and pulling the Ford into a thick stand of trees so you couldn't see it from the road. I'd packed a ham sandwich, and wrapped a couple of canned Cokes in aluminum foil. I shoved these into my pockets, grabbed a flashlight, and started walking.

Walking the mile back to Delbert's house was not the most fun I've ever had. I wanted to avoid the road—my luck, Delbert would be driving home—so I cut through the woods. It was getting late in the day, and the fading light made it hard for me to see through the trees. All the time I was walking, I was doing some heavy hoping that I wouldn't run into anybody in a similar getup.

I always feel a little uneasy in the woods, particularly around this time of year. It's hunting season. In the autumn months around these parts, you can see trucks driving by and parked out in front of the Crayton

County Supermarket almost every day with Bambi's mother—and sometimes Bambi's dad—strapped across the front.

I'm not much of a hunter myself. Vergil and Elmo have both asked me several times to go hunting with them, but I've always said no. I reckon I'm one of very few around these parts who doesn't have a gun rack on the back of his truck.

I guess that makes me an oddball. I've only shot one thing in my life, and I don't guess I'll ever forget it. It was back in Louisville. I had to shoot a seventeen-year-old kid who at the time was doing some painful things to an elderly store clerk. The clerk had refused to give the kid the money out of the cash register.

I didn't kill the boy, but I can't ever forget how his face looked when that bullet ripped through his shoulder. I don't rightly know how I could ever be a hunter after that.

I guess I just don't understand hunting. And, because I don't understand it, I feel uneasy around it. I feel uneasy for another reason, too. I know perfectly well that there are a lot of hunters out there who are just as careful as anything. But, I also know that all it takes to have some real fun is just one drunk wandering through these woods who shoots at anything that moves.

As I walked toward Delbert's, I tried to move with distinctly un-deerlike movements. Whatever that is. I thought about singing, and decided that Delbert and all his neighbors would probably come out on their porches to find out who in the world was The Happy Hunter out there in the woods.

It took me about fifteen minutes to get to where I was going, what with all the times I stopped and listened for possible drunks walking nearby with loaded weapons. The first thing I noticed when I came out of the trees across from Delbert's house was that the lights in Delbert's living room were on. Either he was so drunk, he'd gone out and left them on, or he'd already passed out, and left them on. Or, possibly, he was still in there. Still home.

I found out right away which one was right. I could see the shadows of two people moving around in front of the drapes. Somebody else evidently was in there with Delbert.

From where I stood, I could see the back of a red pickup. It had been parked all the way in back of the house—so I couldn't see it real well—but it was a truck all right. I was sure it hadn't been there when I'd visited Delbert before.

I settled myself behind the largest, thickest shrub directly across from the house, and started drinking one of my Cokes. After a while, I noticed something.

The mosquitoes were still pretty bad even though it was September. My ham sandwich must've attracted them. Or maybe as soon as I sat down, the mosquitoes had put out an all-points bulletin. Edible Human in Junglewear Dead Ahead. I was pretty sure that every inch of skin on both my arms had been completely chewed up when Delbert's front door swung open.

Walking out, carrying a large, green plastic garbage bag, was Joe Eddy.

Shrinking back lower behind the shrub, I stared at him. What was he doing here? Somehow, I doubted that Joe Eddy had driven all the way into town to help Delbert take out his trash.

Although, Lord knows, Delbert could certainly use the help.

CHAPTER

TWELVE

Joe Eddy stopped and looked around real carefullike, with the garbage bag dangling at his side, before he continued heading toward the back of Delbert's house where the red pickup was parked. He needn't have bothered. After all, the nearest building was the Crayton County Supermarket, and Delbort's house was set too far in back of the store for anybody to see anything from there.

The garbage bag Joe Eddy was carrying looked to be about half full of something. I stared at it, trying to figure out what on earth could be in there. What would look that soft? It looked like he was carrying a big sack of cotton candy.

I didn't have much time to look at the sack, though, because right after Joe Eddy came Delbert, banging the front door behind him. Delbert was walking with the characteristic swaying shuffle of someone with three sheets to the wind.

"But, Joe Eddy, I'm the one taking all the chances,"

Delbert was saying, his voice slurred. "Unnerstan'? I should be getting as big a cut as you."

Joe Eddy stopped dead in his tracks, then turned slowly to look at Delbert. He looked like a big grizzly about to swat a fly. "Oh no, you shouldn't get as much as me," Joe Eddy said. "Because I got the most to lose. I got me a house and land and everything. And you—you ain't got nothing. You hear?"

Delbert would've had to have been deaf not to hear Joe Eddy. His voice boomed all the way across the road to where I was sitting, motionless, crouched in the shrubbery, trying not to scratch. The mosquitoes in my immediate vicinity were having themselves a field day. For a second there, I thought for sure I could hear their high, tinny laughter.

Delbert, however, apparently didn't catch every nuance of Joe Eddy's meaning because the old man said, scratching his head, "But, Joe Eddy, you know this ain't fair. It should be a fifty-fifty split." Delbert's argument lost some of its force because he was backing up a little even as he spoke.

Joe Eddy took a step toward Delbert, raised the garbage sack to where it was level with Delbert's eyes, and gave the sack a vicious shake. It didn't take a whole lot of imagination to picture him doing the exact same thing to Delbert's neck. "Look," Joe Eddy said through his teeth. "I could get me another partner. If you ain't happy."

Delbert, even in his intoxicated state, apparently still had a functioning imagination. Instantly, he put on a happy face. "Oh, no, Joe Eddy, I—"

I didn't hear the rest. The two of them were going around the side of the house by then, out of earshot.

I started swatting mosquitoes and scratching like crazy the second they were out of sight. I didn't get to scratch for long, though. A minute later, Joe Eddy pulled out of the driveway. Right after that Delbert came shuffling back around the side of the house. When he got to the front door, he gave the frame a quick kick, and said, "Shit."

That door frame didn't look as if it could stand too many kicks like that one. Delbert, however, didn't look as though he cared. He went on inside, slamming the door behind him.

I'd seen enough. Also, I was sure I'd donated enough of my blood to the Mosquito Foundation. I picked up the remains of my sandwich, put my empty Coke can back in my pocket, and headed back to my truck.

On my way home I stopped by Higgin's Stop 'n' Shop for something to spray on bug bites to make them stop itching so bad. All the time I was driving home, squirting my arms with the stuff, I kept thinking about what I'd just seen.

Obviously, Joe Eddy and Delbert were in some kind of business together. What do you know. After what Delbert had told me about not even seeing Joe Eddy at all anymore, too. That old man had actually lied to me. What a shock. It was getting to where you couldn't trust anybody anymore.

This is something I tried to explain to Claudzilla when she called me up from Louisville that day. I told her that I keep trying to think the best of people— and they keep proving me wrong. It's a damn shame.

Apparently, judging from the way Joe Eddy and Delbert seemed to be sneaking around, the business the two of them were in didn't seem to be the sort that was going to be written up in the *Wall Street Journal*. Could this have been what Grammy had been talking to Beatrice about at Ray Don's funeral? Maybe Grammy had known about whatever it was that Joe Eddy and Delbert were up to, and it had gotten her killed.

Of course, that didn't exactly explain why the pets had been murdered, too. Although, if Delbert had decided Grammy had to go, maybe he'd also decided to kill the pets, too, on impulse. Because he'd always disliked them so much.

My next step was pretty clear. I was going to have to search Joe Eddy's place. Whatever the big guy had been carrying in that plastic garbage sack would probably be on his property somewhere. The first place I intended to look was that barn in back of his and Eunice's house.

The best time to search the place would have to be late at night, after everybody was sure to be in bed. That meant I wasn't going to get my full eight hours in tonight. It also meant I was going to have to do something about Hector, Joe Eddy's dog from Hell. I had no intention of becoming Hector's midnight snack.

It wasn't any big mystery what I would have to do. About two years ago, a dogcatcher friend of mine had gotten me a tranquilizer gun. It was during the time I was working undercover as a mailman in Louisville. You know all those jokes about dogs and mailmen? I found out the first week they weren't jokes. My trusty tranquilizer gun ought to be just the thing to put a smile on Hector's face.

Speaking of dogs, Rip was ecstatic, as usual, to see me. Jumping at me, wagging his tail, barking with joy. I would've been a lot more moved by Rip's hysterical greeting if I didn't know that he would still act like this if I'd been gone just five minutes, instead of a couple of hours.

I changed into the dark green jogging suit I sometimes sleep in, fixed myself another ham sandwich, and was just setting my clock for 2:00 A.M. when Rip started carrying on again. That dog is better than a doorbell—being as how a doorbell doesn't come in and bark at you if you don't answer the door fast enough.

For a minute there, I thought maybe Vergil had started feeling bad for acting the way he'd acted earlier. And that maybe he'd come by to dust for fingerprints after all. I headed for the front door, Rip at my heels not only barking now, but growling a little.

It wasn't Vergil, however, standing out there on my deck.

It was Cordelia, looking even prettier than usual in a bright red shirt and a denim skirt. Unless I missed my guess, Cordelia was also looking a tad bit anxious.

"Why, this is a real pleasant surprise!" I shouted, holding the door open for her. I had to shout because Rip was still barking his head off right in back of me. "Rip! Quiet!"

Rip kept right on. He tried out a couple of snarls. I think that dog really enjoys moments like this.

Cordelia looked over at Rip uncertainly, but she gave me one of them dazzling smiles of hers, anyway. "I just thought I'd drop by!" she yelled over Rip's barking. She made no move to come inside, her eyes darting from me to Rip.

"How nice!" I shouted even louder. I looked back over at Rip. "Rip! *Shut up!*"

Rip apparently wasn't about to let me think I was in charge. It might go to my head. He barked a couple more times just for good measure. Then, his point obviously made, he concentrated on wagging his tail.

Once the tail-wagging started, Cordelia stepped into the room. "Oh, isn't this nice," she said, looking around.

My living room is not quite the Bermuda Rectangle
that Melba would have you believe that my office is,
but the two places have definitely been done by the
same decorator. Like my office, my living room has a
lot of magazines and newspapers tossed around. And
more than a few dog toys on the floor.

It is, however, nowhere near as bad as Delbert's. I
do draw the line at leaving decaying food lying around.

Cordelia, though, had never seen Delbert's, so there
was a real good chance she couldn't fully appreciate
the difference between our two places. When she said
that about it being so nice in here, she was looking
straight at a large rubber dog toy in the shape of a
sirloin steak lying in front of my wood-burning stove.
That particular dog toy had been gnawed real bad.
Somehow, I doubted Cordelia's sincerity.

Cordelia gave me another bright, nervous smile,
and then just kept standing right inside my front door,
looking around. Rip took this as his big chance to do
what he always does with guests.

He sniffed her shoes.

"Okay, Rip," I said, "that's enough." Rip ignored
me, and continued sniffing—starting to work his way
up Cordelia's leg—until I gave him a sharp tap on the
head. Rip blinked, gave me a reproachful look, went
over to his favorite chair, and laid down in front of it.
Sulking.

Cordelia had not moved a muscle during the entire
shoe-sniffing ordeal. Either she'd been frozen with
fear, or she'd decided that making any sudden move
around Rip was probably not a good idea.

"You don't have to worry about Rip," I said. "He
wouldn't hurt a fly."

"But I'm not a fly," she said, looking over at Rip
anxiously. When he heard his name, Rip lifted his

head and panted at us, his mouth opening in a big grin.

Cordelia started when Rip's head went up, but after he made no further move in her direction, she seemed to calm down some and moved on into the room.

I've got me one of them wrap-around couches against one wall, and I'm using a big wooden wire spool turned on its side for a coffee table. I like it because it can hold two whole layers of magazines, one on top and one around the bottom.

Cordelia evidently decided, what with the magazines and newspapers and all, there wasn't enough room on the couch for her to sit down. She chose one of the navy plaid chairs I've got on either side of my console TV. "This is really nice," she said again, her smile every bit as bright as her red shirt.

I smiled back, and sat down on the couch, moving a couple of the magazines to the pile on the wire spool. Was I getting paranoid? Or was something up?

"So," Cordelia said, "aren't you even going to offer me a drink?"

I jumped up. "Oh. Sure," I said. Smooth as always. "What would you like?"

Inwardly, I cringed. I'm not much of a drinker myself. Just a beer occasionally. I know nothing about making fancy drinks. If Cordelia said anything other than wine or beer, I was going to have to ask her to make it herself.

"Oh, how about a gin Collins?"

I just looked at her. The screen on my TV probably looked less blank.

"Would you like me to make it?" Cordelia asked. She got up and almost ran into the kitchen. Either she wanted a drink real bad, or she was pretty anxious to get out of the same room Rip was in.

Things seemed less awkward after that, though. In fact, while Cordelia was bustling around in my kitchen, going through my cabinets, looking for stuff to make her drink with, I actually thought maybe this really was just going to be a social call more than anything else. Maybe I really was getting a little paranoid when it came to women.

I was also starting to think that maybe I could go search Joe Eddy's place any old time. Tomorrow night, even.

Cordelia finally got her drink fixed. I didn't have the stuff for whatever she'd said before so she settled for a Bloody Mary. I got me a beer, and we both went back out to the living room.

I did notice that Cordelia immediately glanced toward Rip. He looked as if he were asleep.

"I guess you're wondering what I found out from Ray Don's neighbor," I said, sitting down on the couch again. "It was real interesting—" I started right then to tell her what all Beatrice had told me, but I reckon I hadn't said ten words when Cordelia held up her hand.

"I didn't come over here tonight, Haskell, to talk about Ray Don Perers' neighbor." She still hadn't sat down again. She was just standing there in the doorway to the living room, watching me.

"You didn't?" I said. I took a sip of my beer, watching her. Of the two of us, I had no doubt that I was having the better time.

Cordelia followed my lead, and took a sip of her Bloody Mary. "I feel real bad about what's been happening to you—" she said. She moved then to sit right next to me on the couch.

I can't say I hated the direction things seemed to be headed in.

"And I like you far too much to be causing you so much trouble." Here Cordelia paused, then leaned over and kissed me. Long and hard. I had the good sense to put down my beer when I saw her lips headed my way, or I probably would've dropped the can right on the floor.

For a while I didn't do anything but enjoy kissing Cordelia. She'd put her own drink down, too, after that first kiss, so we both devoted our full attention to touching and kissing and getting as close as we could to each other.

Unfortunately, Rip apparently wasn't asleep after all, and I guess Rip began to feel left out. After a while he came over and stood at the corner of the couch. I was otherwise occupied so I didn't even notice him.

Until Rip barked at us.

He barked just once, but it was real loud, and real unexpected. Cordelia jumped, her bottom teeth hitting my upper lip at exactly the same time as my top teeth bit into her bottom lip.

It was not a romantic moment. It was, however, a moment in which I wondered why I was so glad Rip had been spared this morning.

For a second Cordelia and I didn't do anything, except look at each other and hold our mouths. Then we looked at Rip.

"Bad dog, Rip, bad dog," I said, pointing a finger at Rip. He hates that. I reached over to grab his collar to haul him outside. Rip ducked away, pushing up the sleeve of my jogging suit, and ran over to hide behind one of my plaid chairs.

"Oh my goodness," Cordelia said, her eyes growing larger when she saw all the mosquito bites on my arm. "Are those flea bites?" She moved a little away from me, smoothing down her skirt.

I smiled at her. Real calm. Rolling the sleeve back down. "Oh, no, those are just mosquito bites. I was out in the yard a spell tonight, and the mosquitoes were real bad."

Cordelia apparently did not take my word for it. "You know," she said, her big blue eyes focused worriedly on Rip, "when you keep a dog indoors, you get fleas all over everything. In the carpet, in the upholstery, everything." She waved her hands to encompass the entire house. "They lay eggs, you know. *Hundreds* of them, all over."

"No kidding," I said. I tried not to think about how much Cordelia was suddenly reminding me of my ex-wife. Being married to Claudzilla was like being on a lecture circuit. *Her* lecture circuit. "Well, maybe I better put Rip outside."

I started to get up to do that very thing, but Cordelia's hand on my arm stopped me. "No, you don't have to do that," she said.

I thought she meant that she really didn't mind having Rip inside all that much. I'd already begun to smile when Cordelia went on. "I—I really can't stay much longer. I just stopped by to—to tell you how upset I am. About your tires getting cut up and all. And about somebody trying to kill your dog." Her big blue eyes looked all shiny and soft with emotion. "It—it really is awful."

I was touched. I felt real mean, even thinking for a split second that Claudzilla and this sweet woman could have anything—anything at all—in common. "Why, that's real kind of you, but you don't have to worry—" I said.

Cordelia interrupted. "Oh, but I do. I worry about

you a lot." She swallowed and looked away. "And that's why I'm taking you off the case."

I couldn't help it. My mouth dropped open. When I could speak, I said, "You're *firing* me?" I had never been fired before in my life.

Cordelia looked back over at me and smiled. I think she probably meant it to be a gentle sort of smile. I thought it looked real condescending. "Now, Haskell," she said, "I don't want you to think of it as being fired."

No? How was I supposed to think of it? As just not having a job?

Cordelia reached over and touched my cheek. "I just don't want you getting hurt." She gave me a tender smile. "You're too special to me to have you taking risks like this. I really do wish now that I had just left this whole thing in the hands of the police."

Well, now, Vergil was going to be elated. That was for sure.

"I want you to give me a bill for your time and expenses up to now." Cordelia pointed a long, slender finger at me. "And you be sure to include the cost of replacing your tires."

I nodded weakly. Being fired was everything it was cracked up to be. A load of laughs.

Cordelia was on her feet now, turning toward the door. "Look, I'll call you tomorrow," she said. "Okay?"

What could I say? Of course not? If you think I'm quitting this case, you're crazy?

"Okay," I said, smiling. I even kissed Cordelia when she leaned toward me at the door.

As soon as she was gone, though, I went into my bedroom and just sat there on the bed. Rip followed me, but he didn't come in. He knew there was a good chance that I might still be mad at him, and he wasn't taking any chances. He just sat there in the doorway watching me think.

Was I being too negative, as Claudzilla said, or was Cordelia's new-found affection for me a little hard to believe? I mean, I know I'm adorable and all, but this *was* a little sudden. It generally takes a little time for a woman to succumb to the old Howdy Doody charm. So, if this was indeed an act tonight, then the question was why? Was Cordelia really protecting *me?* Or was she trying to protect someone else?

Maybe she'd found out about Joe Eddy and Delbert's partnership and decided it would hurt Eunice too much if her husband was caught doing something illegal.

And yet, that didn't make sense. Cordelia didn't like Joe Eddy, and she'd told me she wished Eunice would leave him. Joe Eddy going to the slammer might certainly hasten Eunice's leaving the big guy. No, I really didn't believe that Cordelia would lift a finger to keep Joe Eddy out of trouble.

So what was up? Had Cordelia found out that Grampap had really murdered Grammy after all, and she was trying to call me off before I found out, too? Or was she protecting someone else?

Then again, maybe Cordelia had been threatened herself. Maybe she was running scared.

I checked the alarm on my clock: 2:00 A.M., that's what it said. I laid down on the bed, determined to get a little sleep if I could.

Because whether I was working for Cordelia—or working for myself—I was still going to find out what Joe Eddy and Delbert were up to. There was too much cop left in me to let that one go.

As soon as I lay down, Rip must've decided it was

safe. He padded into the bedroom, and settled himself down at the foot of my bed.

It seemed like ten seconds later when the alarm went off. I must've jumped a foot. At the end of my bed, Rip barked once at me, clearly annoyed at having his beauty rest interrupted.

I shut off the buzzer. For a second, I couldn't remember why in the world I'd wanted to wake up at this ungodly hour in the morning.

Then, of course, it all came flooding back.

I got up, stretched, and turned on the lamp. Then I went over to the closet, and reached up to the top shelf.

I hated to do this, but if I was going to have a look-see at Joe Eddy's, I was going to have to carry something a little more substantial than a flashlight. Just in case.

Standing there in the night, with Rip looking at me as if I were out of my mind, I loaded my gun.

CHAPTER
THIRTEEN

Bouncing over all the potholes on the road to Joe Eddy's house was even more fun in the dark than it had been in broad daylight. For one thing, you could hardly see any of the potholes far enough ahead to even try to dodge the things. I was sure several of my back teeth had been jarred loose by the time I finally decided to cut my lights and pull off to the side of the road.

I could see Joe Eddy's house up ahead. Somebody had left the porch light on, and it made a white oval on the front yard. I couldn't see any other lights, at Joe Eddy's or at Grampap's next door. I couldn't see Hector anywhere, either.

I was still pretty far away, though, so that didn't mean anything. Hector was probably hiding under the porch, hoping to lull me into a false sense of security before he went for my throat.

I started loading my pockets with everything I'd brought with me. I'd changed into a T-shirt and blue jeans, and put on a denim jacket so I'd have more pockets to carry stuff in. Into one jacket pocket I put a flashlight, into the other my gun.

In the front pocket of my jeans, I put a pair of wire cutters and a screwdriver, in case I ran into any locks. In the other pocket, I put a sirloin steak, wrapped in Saran Wrap, that I'd taken out of my refrigerator just before I left.

This last, I must say, felt real strange in my pocket. It felt as if I were carrying around an extra lung.

The steak, however, was a real necessity. It was my back-up plan. I intended to throw the steak at Hector if my tranquilizer gun didn't work. I hadn't fired the gun in a couple of years, and I wasn't absolutely sure it would still do the trick.

If it didn't, I didn't want to have to hurt old Hector. He was just a dog, doing his duty. It probably wasn't even Hector's fault that he was so bad-tempered. If I had to spend my days with Joe Eddy, I might snarl some myself.

I really hoped the tranquilizer gun worked. Before I'd left the house earlier, I had been tempted to try the gun out on Rip—particularly in light of how he'd acted earlier this evening with Cordelia—but I decided that tranquilizing Rip might be a big mistake. He might enjoy it so much, he'd want me to shoot him up every night.

That's all I needed. An addicted dog.

I started walking through the woods toward Joe Eddy's, carrying the tranquilizer gun in my right hand, ready to pull the trigger at the first sign of Hector the Horrible. Once I was well off the road, and away from the front of the house, I got out my flashlight. I sure needed it. Even though the moon was almost full, it was as dark as the inside of a refrigerator in among those trees.

I reckon I was thinking about the insides of refrigerators because of what I was carrying around in my jeans. Every time I moved my legs, I was rudely reminded that there was a damp, cold package in my front pocket.

Halfway there, I came to a definite conclusion. Steaks are not meant to be carried around on your person.

My plan was to walk a large imaginary circle around Joe Eddy's house, so that if Hector was going to jump me, he'd do it well away from the house. My imaginary circle ended right behind the ramshackle barn in back of Joe Eddy's place.

I walked slowly, giving Hector all the time in the world to show up, but nothing happened. When I finally got to the barn door, I stopped, listening.

All I could hear were crickets.

I kept the tranquilizer gun pointed into the darkness, and moved to the barn door. There I stopped and listened again.

Nothing. No growl, no bark, no nothing.

Maybe Hector was inside tonight. I reached for the door latch and unhooked it. Surprisingly, the barn door wasn't even locked or anything. Joe Eddy must feel real safe all the way out here. I was beginning to suspect that I'd brought all this stuff with me for nothing. I was also beginning to suspect something else.

I hadn't wrapped the steak carefully enough. It was dripping down my leg.

Oh joy. I'd turned off my flashlight once I got close to the house, but even by the light of the moon, I could plainly see that there was now a large dark stain on the front of my jeans. It didn't look as if I'd be called upon to give any lessons on personal hygiene in this outfit.

I opened the barn door just a crack and eased myself inside. Even without the flashlight, I could've seen the large vehicle parked right in front of me. Turning on the flashlight, however, told me that the large vehicle was a brand-new, fire-engine red Corvette.

Well, well. It sure looked as if Joe Eddy-Delbert Enterprises had been doing real good. I moved the flashlight around, and immediately spotted what I'd come here to find. Leaning against the walls of the barn all around me were large, green plastic garbage bags. Most of them looked chock-full.

I went over to the closest one, and untwisted the twist tie that held the bag closed. As soon as I got that bag open, I knew what it was.

Nothing has quite the same musty, sweet smell as marijuana.

The first bag I opened was filled almost to the top with dried leaves. Then, as my eyes adjusted further to the light, I could see that quite a few pot plants were hanging above me, still drying out.

Judging from all the bags stacked around me, I would guess that old Joe Eddy had had himself a banner year. This was, no doubt, why Joe Eddy had been so willing to move all the way out here in the first place. He sure hadn't seemed like the type to up and move, just because his wife was concerned about her aging grandmother. He did, however, seem like exactly the type who would up and move in order to go into the pot-growing business.

Joe Eddy evidently headed up the agriculture end of the business, while Delbert took care of sales. I looked around and smiled. *Well, boys,* I thought, *your business is about to take a fiscal nose dive.*

I'd seen all I needed to. I was just turning to leave, when the barn door in back of me was thrown open. It was opened with such force that the door slammed into the front of the barn with a sound like thunder.

Standing in the doorway, looking about as cheerful as a thunderstorm, was Joe Eddy. The first thing I noticed about him was that he was holding a shotgun. The second thing I noticed was that it was pointed unwaveringly at my chest.

Bringing up the rear was, of course, Hector, barking to beat the band. The dog had apparently come tearing out of the house right behind Joe Eddy. Once Hector got to the barn, however, the dog stopped.

With Joe Eddy filling the doorway, Hector didn't dare try to run around him. Stymied, the dog kept lunging forward, then dancing back, then lunging forward again. You could tell Hector really wanted to scoot past Joe Eddy and head for a quick snack on my ankles, but he was afraid to get too close to Joe Eddy's feet.

"What are you doin'?" Joe Eddy said to me.

Only Joe Eddy would need an explanation.

"I was just admiring your new car," I said.

Joe Eddy's eyes turned into little slits. "You funnin' with me?" He tightened his grip on the shotgun, and took a couple of steps forward. He was wearing blue striped pajama bottoms, a V-necked undershirt, and untied work boots with no socks. Either Joe Eddy had dressed in a hurry, or he was starting a whole new look in bedroom wear.

"Oh, no, Joe Eddy, I'd never do a thing like that," I said. "I'd never do any funnin' with you." I was thinking fast, looking around us, trying to figure a way out. The inescapable conclusion seemed to be: There wasn't any.

"Put that there gun down." Joe Eddy indicated the tranquilizer gun I still held in my hand. I had considered trying to shoot him with it, but I wasn't sure it would go that far. I also wasn't any more sure of the gun now than when I was thinking about using it on Hector. If the gun didn't work, I was pretty sure it wouldn't help to throw Joe Eddy the steak.

Although it was a thought.

A short, high scream made both me and Joe Eddy look back toward the door. Standing there, barefoot, in a pink-flowered flannel nightgown, was Eunice. Her face was white as death, and she had both her hands over her mouth, as if she were trying to stifle her own scream.

Joe Eddy looked downright annoyed.

"What—what's going on?" she asked, looking from me to Joe Eddy, and back again.

I thought I'd let Joe Eddy handle that one.

"What's it look like?" Joe Eddy said.

So much for him explaining everything in detail. "I believe I've found out what your husband really does for a living," I said.

Eunice's eyes widened, but you could tell that what all I'd just discovered in that barn was not exactly news to her. "Oh God, Joe Eddy, I knew you shouldn't do this," she said, her voice shaking. She turned back to me. "I tried to tell him, but he wouldn't listen—"

I really wished Eunice wouldn't go into this right now. Joe Eddy was looking like a grenade whose pin had just been pulled. "Shut *up!*" he yelled.

Eunice must've jumped a foot. She did, however, take Joe Eddy's advice.

Hector did, too. He'd been barking off and on, but now he settled for a low-pitched growl.

"Now, Eunice," Joe Eddy said, "you get over there and see if Haskell's got any more weapons on him."

For a second Eunice didn't move. She just stood there, motionless, as if she hadn't even heard him.

"Eunice!" Joe Eddy sounded just about out of patience. Something I doubted he'd had a whole lot of, right from the beginning.

Eunice jumped again, just as if Joe Eddy had slapped her. She started walking toward me, moving as if pulled by invisible strings, her eyes already apologetic. *I'm so sorry, but I've got to do what he tells me,* her eyes were saying. *I'm so, so sorry.*

Lord knows, I was, too.

She felt the sides of my jacket, and looked back over at Joe Eddy. "He's got something in his pockets," she said. She pulled out the screwdriver and showed it to Joe Eddy.

Joe Eddy shrugged, and said to me, "Take that jacket off, and give it to Eunice."

So much for trying to go for my gun. I did as I was told, and handed the denim jacket to Eunice. She took it, holding it as if she were afraid it might break, her eyes very big.

Once I took the jacket off, you could see real plain the dark stain on the front of my jeans. Joe Eddy looked at it and snickered. "You're scared shitless, ain't you?"

Now, this was humiliating.

I held up my hands. "Nope," I said. The "scared" part was true, all right, but I drew the line at "shitless." "As a matter of fact," I went on, trying for a casual tone, "I got me a steak in my pocket. It's leaking real bad."

Joe Eddy snickered again, even louder. "Oh, sure,"

he said. He moved closer to me. That shotgun he was holding seemed to fill the entire barn. "Come on, Haskell. Let's us go on into the house. I got to make a phone call."

I decided going into the house wasn't something I wanted to do. I didn't budge. "No, really," I said, "I do have a steak in my pocket."

"Oh, yeah?" Joe Eddy said. "Let's see it." He looked over at Eunice as if to say, watch me, I'm calling this guy's bluff.

Eunice didn't seem to be impressed.

I pulled the steak out then, moving real slow so Joe Eddy didn't get any more nervous than he already was. I held it up, showing it to him and Eunice both. And, of course, to Hector.

Joe Eddy looked dumfounded. Hector, however, had a completely different reaction.

Old Hector was apparently a connoisseur of good beef. That silly brown dog went nuts, barking and growling and tearing straight toward me, eager to wrench that steak right out of my hands.

Joe Eddy must not feed Hector any too good.

In the process of going for the steak, Hector ran right through Joe Eddy's legs. Which caused Joe Eddy to say, "Hey!" and do a little two-step. Even more important, it caused him to take his eyes off me for a second.

This was what I'd hoped for. I saw my chance and jumped straight toward Joe Eddy, intending to wrench that shotgun out of his hands while his attention was diverted. Why I did such a stupid thing is beyond me, because even as slow as Joe Eddy was, he wasn't *that* slow.

I noticed that right away. Joe Eddy caught on pretty quick to what was going on, and pulled that gun right out of my reach. That wasn't hard for him to do, since so much of Joe Eddy was out of my reach already.

Then, of course, being as how I'd made him so all-fired mad for even *trying* to get away, Joe Eddy evidently thought he should teach me a lesson by bringing the shotgun butt right down on top of my head.

I saw it coming and dodged, so instead of the gun butt hitting me square and no doubt cracking my skull like an egg—the gun glanced off my left temple.

I found out something that instant that I've wondered about, but never really wanted to know. You really do see stars. Little pinpoints of light danced merrily in front of my eyes just before the world went black.

I don't remember falling, or anything after that, until I woke up facedown on Joe Eddy's living room sofa, feeling sick to my stomach. With the grand-daddy of headaches throbbing behind my eyes.

I had no idea how long I'd been out, but I'd done some pretty good bleeding on Joe Eddy's couch. The upholstery felt warm and wet beneath my face. I decided not to point out this mess to anybody. No use irritating Joe Eddy any more than he already was.

I had to have been unconscious at least a half hour, because that's how long it takes to drive out here from Pigeon Fork. And I saw right away that some-body had just made the trip.

Delbert was standing off to one side of me, facing my way, swaying a little as usual. I reckon Delbert was the phone call Joe Eddy had mentioned wanting to make. "—dunno, you never said nothing 'bout killing nobody," Delbert was saying in slurred tones. From the way he sounded, Delbert apparently thought it was okay to drink and drive. "I dunno if I can go along with—"

Joe Eddy was evidently so mad he couldn't stand still. He paced in front of Delbert, his back to me, waving his huge arms. "Look, Delbert, if we let him go, he's going straight to Vergil. We'll be doing time!"

Delbert whimpered.

Joe Eddy took ahold of Delbert's shoulders. "That's right. *Time*. And the feds'll take my car and my house—"

This last bit of happy news was greeted by a low sob from the corner of the room. Joe Eddy and Delbert both stopped and looked over there. I looked, too. Eunice was sitting on the floor in a corner of the living room, still holding my jacket, staring straight ahead, tears pouring down her face.

Joe Eddy grimaced. "Eunice, you better stop that blubbering. I mean it!" Once again, Joe Eddy was showing the world what a caring human being he really was.

Poor Eunice squeezed her eyes tight and sobbed some more, now without making any noise. It was like watching somebody cry on TV with the sound turned down.

I was feeling pretty uncomfortable myself, lying like a sack of potatoes on the couch. It seemed as though every muscle in my body was hurting, but I decided it probably wasn't the best idea in the world to move right then. Everybody in the room seemed to be ignoring me, and I pretty much preferred it that way. Eunice was sitting directly opposite me, but when it looked like she was about to look me in the face, I shut my eyes.

"But if'n we kill him and we get caught, we could get the *chair!*" Delbert was saying. He shook Joe

Eddy's hands off his shoulders. Which, no doubt, took some doing. "I don't wanna die, Joe Eddy!"

At least Delbert and I agreed on something.

Joe Eddy snorted derisively. "We ain't a-gonna get caught. Why, when they find him, they won't even know who he is. If you help me."

Delbert swayed a little more on his feet, but he managed to say, "Huh?"

Which, I thought, said it all.

"It'll be easy!" Joe Eddy said. "We'll cut off his hands so there's no fingerprints, and we'll knock out all his teeth with a hammer. Then we'll bury his body in another county, and his hands somewhere else. Out in the woods so it'll be years before they find them! And, maybe, they won't never!"

With Joe Eddy's back to me, I couldn't see his face, but I think the pause here meant Joe Eddy had taken the time to smile at Delbert. No doubt, reassuringly. "Look, Delbert," Joe Eddy went on, "I read up on this stuff. They find out who a person is by their teeth, and by their fingerprints. But we'll fool them!"

He sounded real proud of himself for having thought all this up. Joe Eddy probably hadn't read three books in his entire life. Wouldn't you know one of them would be about how bodies are identified?

Lying on the couch, I ran my tongue fondly over my teeth. I sort of wanted to keep those. Not to mention my hands.

Of course, if I were dead, I really wouldn't be needing any of them anymore. I reckon I wouldn't be called upon to do any chewing or, say, applauding. Still, the prospect of being buried in several different places at once didn't exactly appeal to me. It was sure going to make Memorial Day confusing.

The minute Joe Eddy started talking about my teeth and hands, Eunice's head jerked up. I wasn't expecting it, so I was a little slow closing my eyes. I wasn't sure if she saw them open or not.

She must not have, though, because she didn't say anything about it. "Joe Eddy," she said, "are you out of your mind? How could you even think of doing such a thing?" Her wispy little voice was shaking. "Look, you ain't killed nobody yet. Right now all you're looking at is jail. Why, they might even let you off since it's your first offense!"

I could hear Joe Eddy take a long, irritated breath. "Look, woman, I'm handling this. You understand?"

Surprisingly enough, Eunice didn't back down. She got to her feet, and walked across the room to stand right in front of me, fingering my jacket nervously. "Think what you're doing, Joe Eddy," she said quietly. "Nobody has to die. *Think.*"

This probably was not the right approach. Thinking did not seem to be one of Joe Eddy's strong suits.

"You think I ain't been thinking? I got that Emmaline woman off my back, didn't I?" Joe Eddy fumed. He started stomping around again, waving his arms. I looked around for the shotgun. It was kind of hard to do, being as how I had to keep real still. I finally spotted it, though, leaning against the wall right next to Joe Eddy.

Joe Eddy had warmed to his subject. "Them letters Delbert wrote didn't work, did they?" he asked.

At the mention of his name, Delbert hung his head.

"But *my* idea sure worked," Joe Eddy said. "Poisoning Emmaline's cat worked like a charm!"

Eunice gasped. Apparently, up to now, she hadn't been aware of her husband's true talents. "Joe Eddy, you didn't—"

"Of course I did," Joe Eddy said, waving his arms again. "Did you think I was going to let some broad ruin everything? That damn Emmaline would've kept on and kept on until Vergil started sniffing around out here again!"

Eunice looked as if some of her air had been let out. She just stood there, staring at Joe Eddy motionless, while he ranted on. "And, if it wasn't for *me*, Delbert here wouldn't even have known to do Haskell's tires." He glanced over at me, and I shut my eyes real quick. "Not that it did much good. Pesky asshole!"

I believe he was referring to me. Not Delbert.

Eunice evidently hadn't given up yet. "But, Joe Eddy, that don't mean Haskell deserves to die—"

"Shit," Joe Eddy said. "None of us deserves to die, but we're all a-gonna one day, sure as shootin'."

Joe Eddy was a philosopher at heart.

"But, Joe Eddy—" Eunice started to say. She didn't get to finish, though, because Joe Eddy interrupted her.

"Look, it ain't my fault his dog didn't eat the poison!"

No doubt, Cordelia had already told them earlier that Rip was still alive, but Joe Eddy had apparently lost Eunice here. She moved closer, looking at Joe Eddy real puzzledlike. She was standing right in front of me now, so that I was staring directly at my jacket, hanging about eye level. I wondered if the gun was still in my pocket. I also wondered if I would have enough time to shoot before Joe Eddy got to his shotgun and blew my fool head off.

It wasn't the kind of thing I like to gamble with. Lord knows, I'd just made a slight miscalculation a few minutes ago, and I had a bloody head to show for it. A missing head would be a real high price to pay.

"What about Haskell's dog?" Eunice said. Her voice sounded strange now, almost too calm.

Joe Eddy shrugged. "Damn dog didn't eat the poison for some reason. I told Delbert exactly what to do, too—how to poison the meat, and to leave one of his notes—but I reckon that dumb dog just don't like hamburger or something. Wasn't my fault. If that dog had died like it was supposed to, we probably wouldn't be in this mess!"

That was one way of looking at it.

Eunice was having trouble following the gist of this conversation. She stared at Joe Eddy, a muscle now working in her jaw. "*You* tried to kill Haskell's dog?"

"Me and Delbert had to do something," Joe Eddy said. "And if'n that fool dog had eaten the meat like any other dog woulda, Haskell probably woulda been scared off for good. Just like Emmaline." He shrugged again. "Ain't my fault. It was that damn dog."

Joe Eddy's logic was amazing. Apparently, I had Rip to blame for all this. I would have to remember to scold him. Bad dog, Rip. Bad, bad dog.

Eunice took a deep breath, her eyes on Joe Eddy. "Then you won't listen to me?" Eunice asked.

Joe Eddy snorted. "You got that right," he said.

Eunice shrugged her thin shoulders hopelessly, turned and walked slowly back to the corner she'd come out of. Before she started moving, though, she dropped my jacket real casuallike on the edge of the sofa.

Joe Eddy turned his attention back to Delbert. "So— are you in or are you out?"

I had the gun in my hand by then. As I was getting

to my feet, I got one good glimpse of Eunice. She was looking straight at me, her mouth set in a hard, stern line. I knew then. Eunice had known exactly what she was doing all along. She'd known I was awake, and she'd known about the gun in my jacket pocket.

Joe Eddy still had his back to me. He had moved closer to Delbert by then, hovering over the old man menacingly. *"I said,* in or out?"

"My guess is that you're both in," I said, pointing the gun at Joe Eddy. "In prison."

Joe Eddy wheeled around, took one look at the gun in my hand, and let out a roar of rage. He apparently didn't appreciate at all my little attempt at humor.

CHAPTER

FOURTEEN

Joe Eddy! *No!*" I yelled. I was going to tell him not to make me shoot him, but Joe Eddy didn't give me the chance. He lunged for his shotgun.

I pulled the trigger of my gun once, but Joe Eddy didn't appear to notice. Maybe his brain was too slow to register something that happened that quick. The bullet hit Joe Eddy in the shoulder, but that stupid fool kept right on going, trying to grab his shotgun.

There wasn't anything else I could do. I had to pull the trigger again. This time I aimed for his leg. Joe Eddy went down with a yelp of pain.

The whole house shook when he hit the floor. What is it they say about the bigger they are, the harder they fall? Lord knows that's the truth.

I kicked the shotgun out of Joe Eddy's reach, and turned to Delbert. He hadn't moved. It was as if he were riveted to the spot, looking first at the gun in my hand and then over at Joe Eddy, writhing on the floor.

"Delbert!" Joe Eddy screamed. "What are you waiting for? Get him!"

Delbert, however, was in no condition to "get" anybody. He swayed a little on his feet, and said, "I think I'm going to be sick." He did look a tad green. He made his way over to the couch, sat down, and put his head in his hands.

"You fool! You damn old fool!" Joe Eddy had a limited vocabulary of curse words, but in the next half hour—after I had Eunice call Vergil to get on out here with an ambulance—Joe Eddy used every curse word he knew. He yelled first at Delbert. Then, after a while, he started in on Eunice.

For a man who had two bullets in him, Joe Eddy seemed to have an amazing amount of energy left. "How could you be so stupid?" he yelled at Eunice. "Didn't you even check those pockets? Are you the dumbest broad in the world or what?" It never did seem to occur to him that Eunice had set him up. I guess if you're stupid, you just naturally assume everybody else around you is, too.

Eunice didn't say a word back to Joe Eddy. She just ran around getting him bandages and stuff, her lips pressed real tight together. Finally, though, I'd had it. I didn't care if he *was* wounded. "Look, Joe Eddy," I said, "if you don't shut your mouth, I'm going to have to shoot you again."

That, apparently, was the kind of argument that got Joe Eddy's attention.

I knew the minute Vergil and his deputies arrived. It was when Hector started carrying on outside. Evidently, that dog had finished off my steak, and was raring to go. I could hear Vergil cursing the minute his car door opened. He seemed to know a few more curse words than Joe Eddy. This was no surprise.

Vergil must've kicked Hector a good one just as he was getting out of his car, because I heard the dog yelp right away. After that, Hector's barks faded into the distance. The dog must've decided to put some room between himself and Vergil.

After Vergil and the ambulance showed up, Grampap showed up, too. He wandered over from next door, looking bewildered. Eunice had changed into jeans and a shirt by then, and was giving Vergil her account of the night's events. She broke off and immediately ran over to the old man. "Grampap," she said, taking his arm, "you shouldn't be over here."

Grampap was watching slack-jawed while they were working over Joe Eddy. The big guy was screaming once again, every time anybody touched him. "Dammit, that hurts!" he kept yelling. "Be careful, you assholes!"

It took four men to lift Joe Eddy onto the stretcher, and they were straining real good. "What happened, for crying out loud?" Grampap asked, turning to me. "How'd you hurt your head?"

I'd put my gun away, and was leaning against a living room wall, trying not to concentrate on how bad my head hurt. "Joe Eddy helped me with that," I said.

"Was there some kind of accident?" The old man's white hair was standing up all around his head, and, I had to admit it, he looked a lot like Einstein, only without the mustache. A genius, however, wouldn't have been caught dead in the pink polka-dot pajamas that Grampap had on. I had a pretty good idea that Grammy had picked those out for him.

I opened my mouth to tell him all about it, but Eunice jumped in. "It's okay, Grampap," she said, giving me a look. "Joe Eddy just got himself into a little bit of trouble, is all." If you called two bullets and a jail sentence a little trouble, that was a pretty accurate statement.

Grampap didn't look as if he were going to be satisfied with the condensed version Eunice wanted to give him. Particularly when they brought Delbert past us, his hands cuffed behind him.

Grampap's eyes got real big. "What did *he* do?"

I looked at Eunice. "He's going to find out, anyway. You might as well tell him."

She looked as if she might cry. "Now, Grampap, I don't want you getting all upset—"

The old man's eyes got even bigger while Eunice was filling him in. By the time Eunice was finished talking, though, Grampap was actually looking a little relieved. "Oh, my," he said, "I was afraid maybe they'd—they'd—" I knew what he was thinking. Grampap had thought Delbert and Joe Eddy were being arrested for the murders of Grammy and her pets.

Grampap didn't finish what he was saying. He just looked over at me and let his voice die off. I could see now that Grampap had started shivering real bad. I couldn't tell if listening to what Eunice had to say had upset him that much, or if he was just cold. It was getting pretty chilly in the living room now, what with all the people going in and out and leaving the door open. Grampap had left his house without his shoes, too.

Eunice turned to me, her eyes pleading. They were carrying Joe Eddy out to the ambulance right about then. The same four guys who'd put him on the stretcher were lumbering past, straining and groaning, with Joe Eddy yelling his head off in the middle of them. "Look," Eunice said, "I have to go downtown with Joe Eddy now, and—"

I must've looked amazed, because she added, "He *is* still my husband. I—I don't know what's going to happen with us, but right now he needs me."

Eunice was one hell of a lady. I could just imagine Claudzilla following me to the hospital after I'd gotten myself shot committing a crime. Claudzilla probably would've shot me a couple of times herself for good measure.

Eunice hurried on, her eyes flicking over to Joe Eddy and back. "Would you mind making sure that Grampap goes on home? It's too cold for him to be out like this."

She didn't have to ask me twice. Truth was, I was starting to feel a little woozy from the cut on my temple, and I didn't mind a bit getting the chance to sit myself down a while.

One of the ambulance attendants had come over earlier to wash the side of my head and to tell me I needed to get myself checked out at the hospital—to see if I had a concussion or some damn thing. That sounded like real good advice. Before I left, though, there was one more thing I wanted to do.

"Come on, Mr. Turley, the show's over," I said.

Grampap didn't protest. The old man probably was real cold. We walked on over to the Pepto Bismol house, in the side door, right into Grampap's kitchen. I could see right away that he hadn't changed a thing since I was here last. The place was still spotless, and Grammy's gardening stuff was still out on the table.

Grampap walked straight to the kitchen cupboard next to the sink, and took down a bottle of whiskey. Evidently, the events of the evening were just starting to hit the old man. "Want to join me?" he asked.

I was pretty sure that a drink was the last thing I needed with my head hurting this bad, but what the hell. I started to nod my head, but I quickly realized that nodding was a real good way to have an invisible hammer begin to pound behind my eyes. I kept my head perfectly still, and said, "A drink sounds real good."

While Grampap was busy over at the sink getting glasses out of the cabinets and filling them with ice, I moved over to Grammy's gardening table. There was last year's seed catalogue and Grammy's sketch. Just like I remembered.

I opened the catalogue and looked up one of the flowers Grammy had written down. Marigolds, the catalogue said, $1.20 per packet. I had time to check out a couple of the other entries before Grampap came over, a highball glass in each hand.

He looked from me to the catalogue, real puzzledlike, and said, "Something wrong?"

I shook my head no, but realized almost immediately that this was a big mistake. The room did a crazy little dip, and went black.

The next thing I knew I was lying flat on my back, underneath a shiny aluminum light that looked a lot like an upside-down bedpan. And people were poking at me.

They kept poking at me for a day and a half. I kept telling them, "Look, read my lips, I want to go home," but the doctor they'd assigned to me—who, incidentally, looked as if he hadn't even started to shave yet—kept telling me, "Look, read *my* lips. With a head wound like that, you need to be under observation."

The only thing I could tell that he was observing was how high my bill was going. Six hundred and twenty-two dollars and forty-nine cents. That's how much it ended up being. For a day and a half in the hospital.

I didn't even have a concussion. They ran all the tests, and all they found was a big bump on the side of my head. Which I could've found all by myself, thank you, and kept my six hundred and twenty-two dollars. And forty-nine cents.

Vergil came in bright and early Saturday morning, to get my statement, and to tell me what I already knew. Delbert and Joe Eddy were under arrest for trafficking in marijuana. "They're going away for a while," Vergil said, his eyes looking a lot more sorry than I knew he felt.

"How is Joe Eddy?" I asked. It did concern me. I didn't particularly want to have killed the man or anything.

Vergil sighed. From the look on his face, I braced myself for the worst. "Joe Eddy tried to take a nurse hostage right after he got to the hospital, so we had to tie him down."

I reckon shooting Joe Eddy hadn't taught him the lesson I'd hoped it would.

"He'll probably be out of the hospital sometime next week," Vergil said. "Both them bullets he took went clean through." Vergil had evidently told me all he wanted to, because he stood up, getting ready to leave. "Of course, then Joe Eddy'll be taking up residence in jail." Vergil almost cracked a smile. I could be wrong, but it might've been a smile. Of course, it could've been indigestion, too.

"I guess," Vergil went on, "we won't ever have enough evidence on Delbert and Joe Eddy to pin Grammy's murder on them, but at least we got them on something."

I wasn't sure I'd heard right. My head was still hurting pretty bad, and I thought maybe the pain had affected my hearing. "What'd you say?"

Vergil was putting his notebook away, and turning toward the door. "I said, at least we got them put away for a while. Even if we don't have enough evidence to get them for the murder."

I was feeling woozy again. "You think Delbert and Joe Eddy killed Grammy?"

Vergil gave me an infinitely sad look. "Sure do. Don't you? Grammy no doubt found out about the pot business, and they killed her to shut her up."

I tried to ignore the headache pounding behind my eyes. Grammy probably had found out about the pot business. That's, no doubt, what she'd been talking about to Beatrice Offutt at Ray Don Peters' funeral. But that didn't necessarily mean that Delbert and Joe Eddy had killed her.

There were still an awful lot of unanswered questions in my mind. For instance, I still wanted to know how come Eunice looked so scared when I mentioned Ray Don and Myrldean Bleemel.

I didn't feel like arguing with Vergil, though. I watched him walking toward the door, and I didn't say a word.

If I'd felt better, I might've asked Vergil a few things. Like, how did he explain the pets being killed, too? Were the pets like Grammy—did *they* also know too much? I would've loved to have said that to Vergil, but I wasn't feeling good enough.

At the door, Vergil stopped and said, "Take it easy, Haskell. You hear?"

I think that was his way of saying get well soon. I was touched.

Elmo came in a little later that day. The gist of his conversation I'd heard before. It went like this: You're going to get yourself killed. Mark my words. And, incidentally, the drugstore business isn't just a job. It's an adventure. That pretty much covered it.

I half expected to see Cordelia, being as how she was so worried about me less than twenty-four hours ago. For all her concern, though, she didn't see fit to drop by. Oddly enough. It made you wonder about her sincerity.

The visit that did me the most good that day, bar none, was Melba's. She came waddling in about five-thirty that afternoon, wearing what I call her "sunny-side-up dress." It's a dress Melba wears a lot to work. The fabric is a shiny print of big white poppies with round yellow centers. From a distance, it looks as if Melba has been pelted with fried eggs—and that most of them have stuck to the target.

Melba's eyes were almost as big as the fried eggs on her dress when she walked through the door of my hospital room. She was clutching a black patent leather purse to her ample chest, as if the thing were some kind of shield.

The bandage on my head was pretty ugly, I guess, and I probably didn't look any too great. I figured this out when Melba stopped halfway to my bed, and said, "Oh God oh God oh God."

Melba should probably never apply for a candy-striper position. I can imagine how cheerful she'd be in Intensive Care.

I gave her what I hoped was a reassuring smile. "Now, Melba, I'm just fine."

"Lordy, Lordy," Melba said.

"Melba, it's just a little cut."

Melba moved closer and sat down next to my bed. "Haskell," she said, drawing her purse closer, "I never dreamed your job could be this *dangerous.*"

I stared at her. Thinking. Then I turned my head a little more in Melba's direction, winced, and followed that up with a moan.

Melba's face went white.

By the time she left that afternoon, Melba had told me three times that I could only count on her for "secretarial duties." Her tone was aggrieved. "Haskell, I'm real sorry, but I'm just too busy to ever do any questioning or watching folks or anything like that. You understand?"

I allowed as how I did. And I made sure I didn't crack a smile until Melba was out the door.

As soon as the hospital discharged me, I went right home and carried a wildly hysterical Rip up and down the steps, and got him food and water. That done, I headed for Eunice's. I'd had a day and a half to think by then, and I was ready to get some answers.

Hector came running up, snarling, as soon as I pulled up. This time, though, I pulled back my foot, and Hector stopped in mid-bark. Then he just sat there, growling at me. Evidently, Vergil had made an impression Hector wouldn't soon forget.

I walked on up to the screen door, but I didn't have to knock. Eunice was already there, holding the door open for me. "I thought I might be seeing you soon," she said. Her eyes looked real weary.

I stepped inside, and saw Cordelia standing over by the couch. The same couch that had my blood leaking into it a few hours ago. Now I could see that somebody had tried to wash the blood off, but evidently blood doesn't come out all that easy. A light brown stain remained on the sofa cushion.

Cordelia's eyes widened when she saw me. She glanced uneasily over at Eunice, and then said, "Why, Haskell, how are you doing? We've been so worried about you."

She was standing in the middle of a bunch of boxes filled, it looked like, with dishes and odds and ends. She and Eunice had obviously been packing.

"You all going somewhere?" I asked, looking from one of them to the other.

Eunice nodded, and took what looked like a well-used Kleenex out of her pocket. "They're going to be taking the house, on account of it being used to grow drugs," she said. "So I'm moving in with Grampap." Her voice was choked with emotion. "He needs me, you know."

Eunice wiped her eyes, and sat down on the sofa, right on top of my bloodstain. "I'm real sorry about what happened to you," she said. "I don't rightly know what to say—"

I sat down in the straight-backed wooden chair I'd sat in the first time I was out here, and I just looked at her. I wasn't real sure what to say either. What do you say to a woman who helped you put a couple of bullets into her husband? Thanks so much? I really appreciate it? "Look—" I said, clearing my throat, "I wanted to tell you that—"

Eunice held up her hand, and shook her head. "I did it as much for Joe Eddy as I did it for you," she said. "I couldn't stand by and let him kill somebody." Her wispy voice sounded stronger today than I ever remembered it being.

I nodded. I was suddenly real anxious to change the subject. "Well," I said, "I guess you're wondering what brought me all the way out here."

Eunice wasn't going to help me out. She just stared at me real blank.

I cleared my throat again. "You know when I took Grampap home? I took myself a good look at that old seed catalogue that's with Grammy's gardening stuff over there." I leaned forward. "Didn't you tell me that Grammy forgot the new catalogue you meant to give her that night? That you still had it over here?"

Something was going on in back of Eunice's eyes, but her glance never wavered. "That's right," she said. "I can show you the catalogue if you want. It's in the kitchen." She sounded very, very tired. I felt almost mean even questioning her. After all, she'd saved my life. And my teeth. And my hands.

"Well, the thing that was bothering me," I said, "was that Grammy had changed the prices on some of the flowers on her list. Some of the flowers had gone up since last year, and Grammy had erased the old price and put in the new." I looked over at Cordelia, because I could hardly stand to see the stricken look on Eunice's face. "How would Grammy have known the prices had changed, if she didn't have the new catalogue?"

Cordelia now looked angry. "Look, Haskell, didn't I take you off this—"

Eunice interrupted her. "It's no use, Cordelia," she said. "He knows." Eunice's voice was as calm as if she'd been talking about the weather. For a wispy-voiced little woman, she had an amazing amount of strength.

Eunice was right, too. I was pretty sure I did know. In fact, I'd had a pretty good idea ever since Eunice said what she did to Joe Eddy, when she was trying to talk him out of killing me. She'd said, "You ain't killed nobody yet." *Now, how did she know that,* I'd thought then. How did she know that Joe Eddy hadn't killed Grammy?

Yep, I was pretty sure I knew who had killed Grammy. What I didn't know, however, was why.

Eunice started answering that one for me right then. "I had to do it," she said, closing her eyes for a second. As if she were trying to blot out the memory. "When I went over there, and I saw what Grammy had just done—and how she acted about it—I'd known then that Grammy was a lot sicker than any of us thought." She shuddered, and then added, "—and then, of course, when Grammy told me about the others—"

I wasn't following Eunice at all, but I just let her talk. She went on and on for maybe the next twenty minutes, talking in a wispy monotone, until I finally understood exactly what had happened that Friday night.

On the way up to bed, Eunice had seen the new seed catalogue still lying on her kitchen table and realized Grammy had forgotten it. She could see that Grammy's lights were still on next door, so she'd let herself out her back door, intending to go next door to give it to Grammy. Evidently, neither Joe Eddy, Delbert, or Grampap heard her leave because they were making so much noise, laughing and yelling at each other over the Rook game.

"When I got to Grammy's back door, I could see her real plain inside, standing there with an iron skillet in her hand. And—and I saw her do it," Eunice told me, her eyes getting big. "I saw her bring that skillet right down on top of Percival's head!"

Eunice was opening Grammy's back door by then,

and when she did, she saw the bird, too, lying very still, inches from Percival's now dead body.

Grammy, however, seemed to be her usual self. According to Eunice, the old woman turned calmly toward her, the skillet still in her hands, and said, "Eunice, look what somebody's gone and done!"

"But, Grammy," Eunice had told her, "I just saw *you* do it."

To which Grammy replied, "Oh." A safe response if I ever heard it.

The old woman shrugged then, and said, "Well, look at what Percival did to poor Sweety-bird. Just look! No wonder I had to do it. He was getting on my nerves real bad!"

Sweety-bird had apparently looked the worse for wear. Poor Eunice was staring at both the bird and the cat, her mind racing, when Grammy said, by way of making conversation, "You know, Eunice, a skillet is real good for getting rid of things. You shoulda seen how good it worked on Myrldean and Ray Don."

This had given Eunice something new to think about. She actually started feeling dizzy, listening to Grammy go on and on about her two deceased friends. "Lands," Grammy said, apparently forgetting what she'd just said, "those two really get on my nerves! Ray Don had the gall to say just last week that his garden was better than mine. Can you believe that man?"

Eunice had then started concentrating on trying not to faint.

"And Myrldean, she told Delbert my coffee was like liquid mud! She said that!" Grammy had moved toward Eunice then, still holding the skillet. Eunice had backed up until her back was against the kitchen door. "I tell you, that Myrldean is really getting on my nerves!"

With Grammy heading her way, Eunice had stifled a scream, but it had turned out that it wasn't Eunice that Grammy was heading toward—the old woman had spotted the new catalogue still clutched in Eunice's hand.

"Oh, you sweet thing!" Grammy squealed. "You brought me your new catalogue!"

Grammy had taken the catalogue right out of Eunice's paralyzed hand, dropped the skillet right on the floor, and moved over to the kitchen table, intent suddenly on planning her garden.

Eunice had watched, her mind no doubt going a million miles an hour. "I was watching Grammy and thinking we should've known something was wrong. Grammy had been forgetting too much lately. She'd even been forgetting to feed Percival and Sweetybird."

No wonder poor Percival had been acting so wild over Christmas. He'd just been anxious for a good meal. This, then, was what had occurred to Cordelia at the restaurant that she didn't want to tell me. Cordelia hadn't wanted to admit to me that Grammy was so out of it, Grammy couldn't even remember to feed her own pets.

"And I was thinking about how Grammy would have to be locked up now," Eunice went on, "—away from her garden and all the things she loved. She'd have to be put away! You couldn't have a little old lady running around killing everything and everybody that got on her nerves."

Eunice did have a point here.

I nodded, and Eunice hurried on. "And I kept thinking how Grammy had taught me all my life about family pride, and about keeping the Turley name

211

clean—and now poor Grammy was going to ruin it all herself!" Eunice wiped her eyes again. "If she'd been in her right mind, Grammy would've died from the shame of it!"

But, of course, Grammy's right mind was among the missing. That was the first conclusion that Eunice had apparently reached, watching Grammy happily drawing on her garden diagram. She reached another conclusion right after Grammy accidentally dropped her pencil on the floor. The old woman picked up her pencil, and then stared thoughtfully at the shiny floor.

"Look at this," she told Eunice, who was at that moment standing transfixed right behind the old woman, "Grampap keeps this floor so clean I don't feel comfortable even walking across it." She pointed her pencil at Eunice. "I tell you, that old man is getting on my nerves!"

Eunice had just looked at her, not saying a word. Grampap obviously was in terrible danger.

"That was when I decided what had to be done," Eunice said. "To protect Grampap, to keep poor Grammy from ever having to spend any time behind bars, and to keep the family name clean. Just like Grammy herself would've wanted."

Eunice took a deep breath. "I—I picked up Grammy's skillet and I did it real quick so she didn't suffer. I did it twice to make sure she—she was gone." Eunice's eyes were round now with the horror of what she was saying. She stared straight ahead, looking at nothing. In back of her, Cordelia wept silently. "And then, of course, I did poor Sweety-bird. So you couldn't tell that the cat had gotten him."

Eunice looked back over at me. "I was afraid if

anybody figured out that the cat had gotten the bird, then they might guess what Grammy had done." She ran a shaky hand through her limp hair. "After that, I washed Grammy's skillet in hot, soapy water, and I put it away."

I tried to look real casual, like I heard this kind of thing every day. But I couldn't help thinking about Grampap right next door. Every morning for months now he'd been cooking his bacon and eggs in a murder weapon. I blinked, and tried to concentrate on the rest of what Eunice had to say. "Then I grabbed up that catalogue, ran back home, and I got into bed. Just like nothing had happened."

Cordelia was sobbing out loud now. "Oh Eunice," she said, "if you'd only told me sooner, I'd never have hired anybody—"

I looked over at Cordelia. "When did you find out?" I asked. I was just a tad curious, that was all.

Cordelia looked away, dabbing at them big blue eyes of hers with a lace handkerchief she'd pulled out of her pocket. "I—I guess it was Thursday. Right after Eunice called you on the phone."

Right before Cordelia had decided she adored me too much to have me work on this case any longer. Why was I not surprised?

No wonder Cordelia had been acting so distracted on the phone right after I talked to Eunice. I'd just asked Eunice about the good catalogue. Eunice must've been looking real upset, knowing that I was getting close. As soon as Cordelia was off the phone, Eunice had no doubt panicked and told her sister everything.

Both Eunice and Cordelia were now looking at me anxiously. "So what happens now?" Eunice asked. She twisted her Kleenex in her lap.

"You're not going to tell, are you?" Cordelia came around my chair and tried to give me one of them dazzling smiles of hers. It looked real shaky. "What good would it do to have all this come out? It would just hurt Grampap. And Eunice and—and me. It would even hurt Grammy. It would be like she died for nothing." Cordelia took my hand in hers and gave it a squeeze. "Please, Haskell, let it go. For me?"

Cordelia really did have the prettiest blue eyes I ever did see.

I pulled my hand away.

CHAPTER

FIFTEEN

These days I see Eunice every once in a while, walking on the street. Or at the Stop 'n' Shop, grocery shopping for her and Grampap, pushing her cart in front of her real shylike, as if maybe she thinks she might be hurting it. Eunice always says hi to me. Or she waves.

Just as if we don't share an awful secret.

I haven't seen Cordelia since that last day. I reckon she went on back to Nashville. I can't say that I care. I reckon Cordelia is one of them women who use their looks to get them where they want to go. I just want to make sure I don't go with them.

Cordelia got real huffy acting that last day when I pulled my hand away and told Eunice, "Okay, but I want you to know—I'm doing this for you and Grampap. Nobody else." Cordelia sort of tossed her head when I said that, and walked out of the room. That woman could make you think real bad of women in general.

I'm working on that, though. So what if there're women like Cordelia and Claudzilla? There're also women like Eunice, who look kind of plain, and talk kind of wispy, and obviously need assertiveness training real bad—and yet, end up being kind of courageous.

As my daddy said, go figure.

Every time I see Eunice, of course, I think about all them clients from all over Crayton County who are not beating down my door. I remember how I solved a big murder case, and I'm not getting any credit for it. Then, of course, Eunice smiles and waves at me. She seems to be looking a lot prettier here lately. Word is, she's leaving Joe Eddy. Finally.

I must say, he doesn't deserve her.

If she got herself divorced, I'd almost consider asking her out myself, but I don't know. I think I might cringe a little every time she picked up a piece of cookware and started making dinner.

I did have one condition before I agreed to keep my mouth shut. I asked Eunice to buy Grampap a brand-new skillet.

These days things are real quiet again. I've been mopping Elmo's floor almost every day. I'm not complaining, mind you.

If I were going to complain, I'd complain about something else: This morning Beatrice Offutt called me up all in a dither to tell me that her granddaughter is finally in town. She said her granddaughter is really excited about meeting a real, live spy.

Like I said at the beginning, it's tough being a hard-boiled detective in a small town.